SHOWDOWN

"Dandy Kilgallen!"

The gambler leaped from the table and backed up with both hands showing plain. The men at the bar turned, and two of them stepped rapidly away as the bartender sank out of sight.

A third drinker recognized the man with the gun. "Hell's fire! If it ain't ol' Charlie Martell—all crippled up and big as life!"

Charlie ignored him. "Kilgallen, I got a warrant fer yore arrest issued from the federal court at Fort Smith, Arkansas. An' I'm takin' you in fer the murder of Nolan Edgewater."

"I didn't shoot nobody," Kilgallen said.

"Drop yore gunbelt," Charlie ordered.

"Hell!" Kilgallen exclaimed. "There ain't no crippled sonofabitch takin' me nowhere!"

We will send you a free catalog on request. Any titles not in your local bookstore can be purchased by mail. Send the price of the book plus 50¢ shipping charge to Tower Books, P.O. Box 511, Murray Hill Station, New York, N.Y. 10156-0511.

Titles currently in print are available for industrial and sales promotion at reduced rates. Address inquiries to Tower Publications, Inc., Two Park Avenue, New York, N.Y. 10016, Attention: Premium Sales Department.

THE
BENT STAR

Patrick Andrews

TOWER BOOKS ⬛ NEW YORK CITY

Dedicated To
JOHN SNOW
A good army buddy and the only guy I ever knew
who could be
a *bon vivant* and sergeant major at the same time.

This book is a work of fiction. Except for well known his-
torical personalities, all characters are fictitious and any
similarity between them and real persons is coincidental
and unintentional.

A TOWER BOOK

Published by

Tower Publications, Inc.
Two Park Avenue
New York, N.Y. 10016

Copyright © 1982 by Patrick Andrews

chapter 1

Thin shafts of the morning sun shot through the cracks in the livery stable walls as Charlie Martell sat up on his bunk. It was a homemade affair banged together out of bits of boards with a dirty straw-filled sack as a mattress, but that was all he could afford.

He dropped his good leg over the bed as he absentmindedly massaged the stiff knee of the right one. The pain in it had been around steadily for the previous five years and he no longer felt the unpleasant sensation as a hurt in that particular joint. It ached in a sort of general way now, his brain at long last accepting it as a permanent part of the body's make-up and no longer alarmed enough to announce the sharp stabs to the conscious mind. A ceaseless throbbing seemed sufficient. The knee itself, stiffened, discolored and swollen into a shapeless unsightly mass of punished flesh and cartilage, had locked itself tighter than the action of a brand new Winchester .44 carbine, which was appropriate since it had been a slug from just such a weapon that had slammed into the knee to cripple it.

Charlie's upper body wasn't much better off. Some .45 pistol slugs had done their job there. The right elbow was solidly locked with a slight bend in it. A town doctor had done that in a thoughtful manner when he set it, figuring it would make it easier for Charlie to handle his horse's reins that way. His right hand was an inoperative claw that couldn't grasp as much as a match anymore. The flesh had smoothed out into a tight whiteness that barely responded to the blood that circulated poorly through the useless, nerveless digits that were drawn up like useless talons.

Charlie stood up and stretched his lanky six-foot frame to rid it of the kinks from sleeping. His face could be described as rugged and handsome if it weren't for the gauntness that dominated the features. His sandy hair was longish and unkempt, showing the disregard he felt for his appearance. As he moved outside in his sort of hop-and-twist gait his whole being was dominated by the need for a drink. The craving he felt for the stinging, warm comfort of whiskey completely overshadowed his hunger.

"Payday, Charlie?" Orv Pickett, the livery operator, grinned at him in gap-toothed contempt from the hay yard. "Gonna git yore handout from the townsfolks?"

Charlie didn't answer. Instead he just glanced at Pickett and acknowledged his presence with his eyes. There had been a time when the pot-bellied sonofabitch had been proud to have a drink with him and had always addressed him as Marshal Martell. But now Charlie was Orv's employee of sorts. At least the livery operator let him sleep in the back in exchange for periodic odd jobs around the place.

"You kin really git likkerred up today, huh?" Pickett asked. "Best day o' the month fer you, I reckon."

"I guess," Charlie said. Then he turned and limped down the street past Webster's Tonsorium,

6

Wichita, Kansas' contribution to the world of barbering. Most people were up and around by then. One benefit of beng a derelict was that he could sleep late without putting too much of a crimp in the day's activities.

"Hey, Charlie!" Sly Webster called from his barbershop.

Charlie stopped and nodded. "Hello, Sly. How you doin' this mornin'?"

"Fine, I reckon. Want a soak? I ain't seen you fer a couple o' days."

"I'll be back later," Charlie answered. "I got to git to the bank."

"Oh, yeah. Payday fer you, huh?"

"Right," Charlie said. "See you in a little while." He made his way down the boardwalk and laboriously negotiated two gaps in it between buildings before he reached the bank. He went into the establishment and hung back from the cages until the people ahead of him had finished their business. Then he went up to the head teller.

"Mornin'," Charlie said.

"Good morning, Mister Martell," the teller, always polite, greeted him. "I'm all ready for you." He reached into his drawer and pulled out a small check-sized document. "Mister Wilcox has signed it, so there'll be no delay." He handed the piece of paper—ten dollars in town scrip—over to Charlie. "There you go, Mister Martell. And I'll see you next month."

"I thank you kindly," Charlie said. He stuck his prize in his pocket to begin his laborious trip back to Sly Webster the barber.

That bit of paper was Charlie Martell's disability pension of sorts. It had been voted to him out of gratitude by the town council after the horrible wounding he received in the line of duty. That, as well as authorization for one meal a day at Preston's Cafe down by the depot, was the sum total for long years of service as a lawman to the community.

Now and then he used to receive a little money, usually five dollars from Nolan Edgewater, but since his old friend had gotten married after his move to Fort Smith, Arkansas, Charlie hadn't heard much from him aside from casual letters.

Sly Webster held the door open as Charlie shuffled into the shop. The barber was genuinely pleased to see him. "I was kinda wonderin' about you, Charlie. Like I said, I ain't laid eyes on you fer a coupla days."

Charlie appreciated the thought." I was just takin' it easy."

"Yo're welcome here anytime . . . you know that, Charlie."

"Sure," Charlie said, allowing what he considered a smile. It was just a slight upturning of one corner of his mouth.

"Alma's been askin' after you too," Sly said, mentioning his wife. "You know what a worrywart she is . . . always sayin' as how one meal a day ain't good enough fer a full growed man."

"Good enough fer a crippled one," Charlie said.

"No it ain't," Sly said. "You know our door's open to you."

"I'll come by tomorrow," Charlie said.

Sly, knowing that payday was Charlie's big night for beginning a drawn-out drunk, accepted that. "Don't you fergit, you hear? Supper with us soon."

"Fine, thank you kindly, Sly. I'll do that."

"C'mon in the back. I got some water all heated up."

Charlie clumped after his friend to the back of the barber shop. There were wooden stalls in the bath area. Each one held a conventional tub except for the last one in the row. There, in all its copper glory, was a large model that boasted even a seat. Charlie, with his injured knee permanently held in its unbendable position, could never have gotten himself into a regular bathub. But the big one had more than enough room for him to settle down comfortably with both legs stretched out in front as he soothed himself in water up to his neck.

The ex-lawman undressed and hung his clothes on the pegs embedded in the stall. Then he pulled himself over the side of the tub and settled down into the lukewarm water already waiting for him. He waited as Sly came back with the first bucket of truly steaming water. The barber poured it in gradually, moving the pail back and forth to distribute the fresh hot water evenly. Four trips later and Charlie was soaking in the steamy bath as it soothed his injuries, easing comforting heat deep into the mangled joints until he felt so good he almost thought he could move his nerveless fingers.

Later that afternoon Charlie was standing at the bar in the Palace Saloon. O'Reilly, the Irish bartender with a perpetually red face, nodded to him, then wordlessly produced several bottles of rye whiskey. Charlie slid the town scrip to him.

"Are you goin' to drink any of it here then?" O'Reilly asked.

"I thought I might relax at a table fer awhile," Charlie answered.

"And it's welcome y'are, but make sure ye stay outta the way," O'Reilly said uncharitably as he handed him a glass.

9

Charlie scuffled to a table near the wall at the far end of the room. He set his burden down and pulled the cork as he settled himself clumsily into the straight-backed wooden chair. He realized the sight of a crippled man with a twisted arm was unpleasant for the customers and perhaps he should resent O'Reilly's reference to his keeping off to himself, but loneliness sometimes outweighs pride in a man, making him long for the company of people even if it is not particularly close or intimate.

There was a time when his appearance in that same drinking establishment would have elicited sudden silence and respectful (if not fearful) glances as he stood just inside the batwings with his right hand resting lightly on the handle of his Colt Peacemaker. He would call out a name and the man he was looking for would always keep his hands in plain sight. Perhaps it was only a misdemeanor charge of disturbing the peace, but no one wanted to tempt Marshal Charlie Martell to draw. Most that did were punk kids or so damned drunk they didn't know any better. The majority ended up buried in the town's boot hill at taxpayers' expense.

"Hi, Charlie."

Charlie had sensed her coming by the waft of strong, cheap perfume that preceded her. He glanced up and gave her his quick, almost unperceivable smile. "Hello, Norma."

She was heavyset with plain, washed-out brown hair that was showing its first gray strands. Her round face was plain and hard, the heavy rouge and lipstick unable to soften the features. She had once left the saloons and married a farmer several years back but had been unable to adapt herself to a one-man life. After several episodes with hired hands

10

Norma was beaten senseless and kicked out. She came directly back to her former life with its degradation and harshness. But her wide grin was genuine and friendly. "I reckon it's payday fer you, huh?"

He nodded. "Want a drink?"

She thought a moment. ". . . Naw, I don't think so. Kinda early yet and that stuff yo're drinkin' is real. I don't wanna git drunk afore the crowd builds up. That sonofabitch O'Reilly'd kick my fat ass fer me."

"How've you been?" he asked.

"Perty good, Charlie. An' you?"

"Same as always."

"I missed you the last time you was here," Norma said.

"I didn't stay long," Charlie said. "I prefer to do my drinkin' alone mostly."

"I ain't botherin' you, am I?"

"Hell, no, Norma. You jest stay there as long as O'Reilly'll let you. We ain't talked fer a spell anyhow."

"They'se a lot you an' me ain't done fer a spell," Norma said. "How come you don't . . . well, come on by and see me."

Charlie laughed a little. "Hell, I only make ten dollars a month."

"Aw, Charlie, I wouldn't charge you nothin' . . . I never did afore, did I?"

"I was a marshal then," Charlie reminded her. "You *had* to be extry nice to me."

Norma smiled. "You never heard me complain, did you?"

"I guess not."

"If'n you ever do come by, well, I reckon I wouldn't mind a bit," Norma said with that enigmatic flash of shyness that saloon girls are able to display from

11

time to time.

"I'll keep that in mind," Charlie said. But he knew he never would. While the slugs that crippled him had slammed into his leg and arm, they did other damage. When a man's pride has been punctured permanently, his manhood goes as well.

A couple of noisy drinkers suddenly burst in through the batwings. Norma glanced over at them and stood up. "I'd best git to work, Charlie. Don't fergit to come callin', huh?"

"I won't fergit," he said raising his glass to her. As she walked away, he suddenly wanted to be off by himself. The thought of being in a roomful of people repelled him. He recorked the bottle, gathered up the others and hobbled out of the saloon for the sanctity of the livery stable.

By the time Charlie was halfway into the second bottle it was dark. He drank slowly and methodically, letting the alcohol's warm glow ease his tensions and push away the feelings of resentment and regret that dominated his sober life. Each throat-burning swallow added to the comfort as he sat there on his bed amid the warmth and smells of patient dumb horses waiting stoically for whatever humans felt they must do with them. Charlie envied their acceptance and ability to endure, wishing with all his heart he had some of those qualities.

Five years before, in 1876, Charlies Houston Martell had been a capable, robust marshal of Wichita. He walked tall and steady through the town; he helped police as he kept a lid on trouble and violence, earning his seventy-five dollars a month (plus one dollar for each arrest) as well as the respect and gratitude of the citizens. But in the summer of that year

12

there was an attempt to rob the local bank and Marshal Martell had intervened, starting a hellacious gunfight that was still the talk of the state of Kansas in 1881.

Charlie had been alone taking his ease and drinking coffee in the marshal's office that morning. The night before had been relatively uneventful with only a couple of drunks arrested on charges of disturbing the peace. It looked like a nice long quiet spell for awhile and Marshall Martell was looking forward to it. But the tranquility of the mood was broken when Ned Darwin, who ran a local dry goods store, slipped into the office with a nervous expression on his face.

"By God, Marshal!" That was all he said as he stood there looking rather ridiculous in his derby hat and white apron. He carried a large, brown envelope in his trembling hands.

Charlie swung his legs down to the floor and eyed him carefully. "Somethin' the matter, Mister Darwin?"

"Well, yes, sir, I think there dang well might be," Darwin said nervously.

Charlie waited a couple of beats, then said, "Fine. Anytime you'd care to let me know . . ."

"I was on my way to the bank," Darwin began. He held up the envelope. "To make a deposit, understand?"

"I sure do," Carlie said caustically.

"Then jest as I approached the door I kinda glanced in the window and things jest didn't look right. No, sir, not right at all."

"What did you see, Mister Darwin?"

"I seen three fellers in there with their guns drawed," Darwin said. He pulled his envelope of

13

money protectively close to his body. "So I turned and hurried over here."

"Yo're sure them jaspers had their guns *drawed?*" Charlie asked, getting to his feet. He pulled his Greener 12-gauge shotgun from its place in the wall rack.

"I'm sure, Marshal," Darwin said.

Charlie stuffed his vest pocket with several loose shells. "You wait here 'til I git back, hear?"

"Yes, sir. I'll do that," Darwin answered.

Charlie went outside and walked down the street toward the bank in quick ground-eating strides. He kept his shotgun hidden as best he could while he maintained just enough speed to avoid attracting attention. If there was a bank robbery in progress he sure didn't want to have a crowd of people hanging around.

He was twenty feet from the bank door when three men walked out. He had seen such hard cases before. They were dirty and rugged-looking from living the primitive lifestyle of the trail, and their demeanor spoke more of the open range than the confines of a town. It was obvious they were trying to appear calm, but Charlie's ingrained senses told him all was not normal. He brought the shotgun up.

"Hold 'er there!" he hollered.

"Aw, shit!" one of the men exclaimed. Then all three reached for their holsters.

Charlie's first barrel exploded and the heavy shot slammed into the nearest man's midsection. The force of the blast threw the outlaw back into one of his partners and both crashed to the boardwalk. Charlie didn't hesitate as the second barrel blew the remaining outlaw through the bank's window. The plate glass broke into large pieces that splattered

14

into tiny bits.

The robber under the dead man was cursing and struggling to free himself from the weight that was pinning him down. Charlie edged up close to him.

"Easy does it, you sonofabitch," the marshal said. He reloaded his weapon. "If I think you're gonna do somethin' too quick to suit me, I'll give you both barrels. You jest ease yore ass outta there."

Strangely the man laughed. "I ain't a damn bit worried 'bout you, Starpacker."

The sudden explosion behind him was simultaneous with the carbine slug that struck deep into the back of his right knee.

Charlie's leg whipped upward and he was suddenly on his back looking into the sky. A further backward glance revealed another man on a horse ready to fire again. One good thing was that it didn't require precision aiming—even when looking at a target upside down. Charlie emptied the saddle with a quick shot that also wounded his attacker's horse. At the same time Charlie was cussing himself for not realizing the gang would have had a lookout or backup man in the street. But the feeling of regret only occupied his attention for a split second. The other outlaw had freed himself from his burden and fired a quick shot at Charlie. It missed, slamming into the boards by his head as splinters spun out of the wood.

Charlie brought the shotgun down and pulled the trigger. But there was no thundering recoil. He had inadvertently used both barrels without realizing it. Another slug hit close to him as he struggled for his pistol. Then his right arm went numb as the bandit at last was able to score a hit. Instinctively Charlie sought his pistol with his left hand, but it was too

15

late. His adversary approached him, grinning wildly.

"Goddamn you, I'll learn you to mess around with . . ."

That was all he said. Several unexpected shots tore into the young man, flinging him through the open window of the bank like a split bag of oats.

Charlie sat up and looked up to see fellow marshal Nolan Edgewater approaching the scene. He had evidently made a quick response to the gunfight and was just in time to shoot down the remaining bandit.

But Charlie had no time to offer his thanks. He was badly hurt and fast sinking into shock. The boardwalk was covered with blood as his mingled with that of his foes. He fainted as Nolan directed several onlookers to scoop him up and rush him to the doctor.

Charlie never could remember much about the following three days. His earliest lucid memory was Doc Hammond sitting on his bed with a sad expression. "They got you pretty good, I'm afraid, Marshal."

He had sensed the seriousness of his injuries and knew that the situation was grave. "Is there a chance o' my not makin' it?"

"You won't die, Marshal, but you won't be the same anymore, either," the physician said as he stood up. "I set that arm of yours so it'll be bent like that permanently."

Charlie felt a mild resentment. "How come permanent? Hell, I got to move the damned thing now and again."

"I bent it so you might wrap your reins around the wrist when necessary," the doctor explained. "It really doesn't matter much. The elbow joint was destroyed and took the nerves with it. You won't be using your right hand for anything."

Charlie looked down at the hand just outside the splint. He touched it once . . . then again, finally pinching it as hard as he could. "Hell, I cain't feel nothin'."

"You won't be able to move it, either," Doctor Hammond said. "You're going to have a stiff leg as well. The knee is as bad as the elbow, but there was no nerve damage. But there's going to be times you'll wish there had been."

Charlie was angry. "Well, goddammit! You fixed me up just fine, didn't you, Doctor?"

"Hell, Marshal! *I* didn't shoot you. You're damned lucky you didn't bleed to death. Some people don't appreciate good work no matter how hard you try!"

As the doctor made his indignant exit, Nolan Edgewater came in. He smiled encouragingly at the patient as he sat down on the bed. "How you doin', Pard?"

"Not too bad," Charlie said with the usual frontier aplomb when discussing sickness or injuries.

"Well, I'm gonna keep a close eye on you," Nolan said. "Fer awhile anyhow. I got that U.S. deputy marshal job down in Fort Smith. Be leavin' in about ninety days when the appointment takes effect."

"Glad to hear it, Nolan," Charlie said. "You been wantin' that fer a long time. I oughta be up and back on the job pretty quick. I might even take time off and visit you down there." Despite his casual attitude, he knew he would have been better off if those bandits had put a killing shot into him. There was no denying the future looked mighty dim at that moment.

17

chapter 2

Charlie Martell was drunk for four days before he finally awoke, sick and gagging, just before noon on the fifth. The empty bottles and disheveled room, along with the door torn off one hinge, gave mute testimony to the confined bender.

He stumped out to the water trough in the livery yard and bent down as best he could to stick his head deep into its cooling contents.

"Welcome back to the real world," Orv Pickett said. He pointed to where the door hung precariously from its frame. "You fix that afore you do anythin' else, hear?"

Charlie looked up with water dripping from his matted hair. "Huh?"

"The goddam door there! Fix it!" Pickett shouted. "An' I got some sweepin' fer you to do too."

Charlie nodded. "Sure, Orv." He pushed himself back up to his feet and groaned through the headache he was beginning to notice.

Orv shook his head. "Damn, Charlie, I'd tell you to straighten up, but I reckon you ain't got much to look forward to 'cept a monthly drunk anyhow. Take yore time with the sweepin'. Tomorrow's as good a time as any."

"I'll take care o' that door then too," Charlie said.

19

"Whatever you want," Orv said disgustedly as he turned to tend to his other more pressing business.

"What day is it?" Charlie hollered after him.

"You was out four this time," Orv answered. "This is Thursday."

Charlie wanted to make sure on that point. That meant he had four meals—not counting that day's—coming from the city. He could double them up and have two feedings a day all through Sunday if he wanted to. Or he could splurge and get in some three a day, but he didn't think that would be wise. It was too easy to get used to and it made it doubly hard to get back to a single supper daily after that.

He limped back to his room and got a clean set of clothes. He changed monthly, washing out the dirty duds following a hot soak at Sly's barbershop. After pulling on his boot—he had noticed he was already wearing one—and getting his hat he shuffled out of the livery yard toward the business section.

As usual Sly Webster was tickled pink to see him. "Howdy, Charlie," the barber bubbled. "I'm all set fer ya. Got some hot coffee a-goin' and the headache powders. You'll be as good as new within an hour. Jest wait'n see."

"I appreciate it, Sly," Charlie said. They went back to the rear and the ex-lawman disrobed carefully. His damned knee always hurt the worst after he sobered up. Somehow he never failed to roll over on it in his drunken stupors, irritating the damaged tissue and ligaments to screaming sensitivity.

"How about a shave today?" Sly asked. "Right after yore bath."

"Sure," Charlie said. This arrangement was almost a ritual with them. Sly seemed to get some sort of pleasure from shaving the beard that sprouted after a prolonged drunk and Charlie, with his own good hand too shaky, was glad to have him do it.

Sly shook the powders into a cup of water and stirred them with his scissors. Charlie took the remedy and downed it in three quick swallows. "Is that coffee ready, Sly?"

"Comin' up," Sly said cheerfully. "Git on in the tub."

The water was cold and Charlie recoiled slightly as he forced himself into it. Sly came back with a cup of coffee in one hand while he toted a pail of hot water in the other. "Sorry the water ain't quite ready," Sly apologized. "I didn't know fer sure when you'd show up."

"Don't mention it," Charlie said, sipping the hot brew as the barber carefully emptied the contents of the pail. He went back for another. Soon Charlie was up to his neck in the warmth he craved as Sly settled down beside him in a chair. "Not much business today, huh?" Charlie asked.

"Naw, Thursdays is always slow," Sly said. He nodded at Charlie's body. "Yore hurts botherin' you much?"

"Enough," Charlie said.

"I reckon," Sly agreed. He started to say something else when the bell tinkled over the door out in the main shop area. "Sounds like a customer. Be back in a bit. You jest enjoy yoreself there, Charlie."

"I'll do that, Sly," Charlie said, wishing he had a cigar. He finished the coffee and gently massaged the aching, puffy knee, letting the injured limb float weightlessly in the soothing buoyancy of the water. He had begun dozing when Sly returned.

"Want a cigar, Charlie? An' more coffee?"

"I'd be obliged," Charlie said, waiting to be

served.

Moments later he drew in on the stogie and exhaled before treating himself to a sip of coffee. Sly had lit up as well and was once again seated beside him. "Say, Charlie, how 'bout tellin' me again how you killed Dan Payton?"

Charlie thought a moment. "Well, that was—lemme think—six years ago. There was a warrant fer Payton outta Missouri and I'd heard he was in Wichita. But I didn't know exactly where. He was supposed to be a gamblin' man so I figgered he wouldn't be too hard to find. So one evenin'—a Saturday it was—I commenced to sorta ease myself in an' out o' the saloons over on the west side there, and I sure enough found him."

"What'd he look like, Charlie? Tell me 'bout that," Sly urged with an eagerness that belied the fact he had heard the story many times before.

"He was tall," Charlie said. "With coal black hair an' a big ol' mustache that kinda turned down 'round his mouth. Payton had them thick ol' bushy eyebrows that slanted up. By God, he was a mean-lookin' man. Devilish, you know what I mean?"

"Oh, I surely do, Charlie!"

"An' he was skinny. Damn, that feller looked like you could hide him down the barrel of a Colt .45. Had him a long, long ol' skinny neck with thick veins in it. They say when he got real mad them veins would stand out like ropes."

"By God!" Sly said, slapping his thigh. "I bet you know that fer sure!"

"That's right. Anyhow, I seen Payton playin' cards toward the back o' the room, so I figgered on gittin' behind him and givin' him a hard rap on the head, then draggin' him on down to the jail. Only

22

trouble was that he had got hisself a chair next to the wall so's I couldn't git in position. But that wouldn't have mattered no how. He seen me—badge an' all—comin' across the room. He stood up and drawed. I was a trifle faster an' got off the first shot. But he cut loose with the second and hit that feller that was clerk over to the stage office. Remember his name?"

Sly thought a moment. "Rogers, or somethin' like that, wasn't it?"

"Prob'ly," Charlie answered. "Don't matter now. He died that instant. At any rate there was a hell of a ruckus what with us shootin', folks yellin' and drunks staggerin' around tryin' to stay outta the line o' fire. And that damned Payton hit two more fellers afore I managed to git one in his chest."

"Knocked him over, did it?" Sly asked.

"I hope to shout. He hit the chair he'd been sittin' in an' flew into the wall. He jest stood there fer a instant with them ol' neck veins a-puffin' out, an' them dark eyes lookin' like they wanted to spit fire at me . . . then he slid down to the floor and kinda sat there as he died."

"What'd he say to you, Charlie? Go on ahead an' tell me," Sly urged excitedly.

"He said, 'You sonofabitch, why'd you have to shoot me when I was holdin' aces full?' "

"Then he died, huh?"

"He did that," Charlie said.

Sly grinned delightedly. "Damn! I like that story. You sure had you a exciting life, Charlie, afore you got laid up."

"I reckon I did," Charlie said.

"Hell, I'm just a plain ol' barber. Cuttin' hair an' shavin' faces, that's all I ever do. An' all I *ever* will do."

"Leastways you won't git all crippled up," Charlie said with conviction. "Don't never forgit that."

"I won't. But, damn, sometimes I git so bored."

"Don't worry none 'bout that. Even after all the excitement I've known, my life sure as hell ain't as good as yours now. Got any more coffee?"

"Sure, Charlie," Sly said, getting up. "But you got memories, Charlie," Sly said over his shoulder as he went to the pot. "That's gotta be worth somethin'."

Charlie thought a moment. His memories spanned thirty-seven years of living. The first few were dulled, tangled recollections of dryland ranches that a hardworking father tried to make pay off—but never did. And there were the usual boyhood adventures on the frontier and the more serious ones as a teenager when guns began playing an important part in his life. During the war he had soldiered in Hood's Texas Brigade and served the lost cause of the Confederacy from start to finish. After the peace he had started back home for Texas once more, but figured he hadn't had much there before the hostilities broke and and he would have less during Reconstruction, so he turned north to Kansas.

Working a farm or ranch was boring after four years of the Confederate army, but he soon found the less routine work of enforcing the law. Abilene, Kansas, had been hiring town policemen to work during the arrival of the cattle drives in that year of 1871. The town marshal was none other than the famous Wild Bill Hickok. Charlie's conduct, coolness under fire and quick decisiveness during trouble caught Hickok's favorable attention and his temporary appointment became a permanent one and he was launched into his career as a professional lawman.

Charlie never did marry. The life of a frontier lawman gave rare opportunities to meet decent women, and on occasion he had lived on the edge of notoriety himself. When a small herd of rustled cattle or horses made their appearance hundreds of miles from their owner it was sometimes more convenient to make deals rather than arrests. One such transaction got a little out of hand and two enterprising cowpokes were left dead on the prairie south of Abilene. Charlie thought it time to move and arrived in Wichita in 1872 after only a year under Hickok's supervision. He had taken an immediate liking to the town and had been on the marshal's staff there for four years when he was gunned down by the bank robbers.

Sly returned with fresh coffee. "How 'bout comin' to supper tonight?"

"Sure, thanks," Charlie said. That would give him five meals due from the city. He was about to have all the food he wanted, and he slipped into one of his rare better moods.

"Did I ever tell you 'bout the time I got jumped by them Mezkin cowboys up in Abilene?" he asked Sly.

"Yeah," Sly answered. "But tell me again, Charlie." The barber settled down to listen with all the excitement and enthusiasm of a child about to hear a favorite bedtime story.

Charlie told the tale with embellishments, drawing out the suspense and playing up an episode which had involved only three young Mexicans feeling too much exuberance from over-drinking after a prolonged cattled drive. When he had finished Sly wanted to hear more, but two customers came in off the street.

The barber reluctantly got to his feet. "Why don't

you drop by at quittin' time? We can go over to the house together."

"I got some things to do," Charlie said diplomatically. He really wanted to give Sly a chance to tell his wife there would be company that night. "I'll be over to yore place 'round seven. Let's fergit that shave 'til tomorrow."

"Fine, Charlie. You gonna leave now?"

Charlie stood up. "I reckon. I cain't spend all day here even if I want to." He stepped from the tub as Sly left, and toweled himself off. After dressing in his fresh clothes he clumped out of the shop—with a wave at Sly—and stopped in the warm afternoon sun. He was in a rare contented mood as he stood there momentarily basking in the warm rays. They felt good, almost as good to his punished body as hot water, so he decided to soak up some of the natural warmth. There was a bench in front of the dry goods store in the next block and he decided to go there and sit a spell.

There was only one person there when he arrived, so Charlie settled down in a good spot and tipped his hat over his eyes and was dozing before he knew it.

"Hey! Hey there!"

Someone was shaking his shoulder. Charlie came awake and looked up. "Yeah?"

It was Ned Darwin, the same man who had come to him about the bank robbery and who owned the store where he was sitting. "Why don't you move on off now? You been here long enough."

Charlie was still a little sleepy. "I beg yore pardon?"

"I want you to git off that bench and move along," Darwin repeated. "Didn't you hear me?"

"What the hell?"

Darwin lowered his voice as two women strolled by and turned into his place of business. "Good afternoon, ladies, I'll be in directly." Then he turned back to Charlie. "I want you to git out o' here, Martell. Ain't nobody want a feller like you hangin' around in front o' his business. You spoil the view. Now git! Or I'll call the town marshal."

Anger swelled up in Charlie in a flash flood of resentment and indignation. "Why you sonofabitch!" he hissed.

Darwin backed away. Even with a cripple he was a physical coward. "I'm goin' fer the marshal . . . right now!" he threatened.

Charlie's face paled further in rage, but he controlled himself and spun on his good heel to scuffle down the boardwalk toward the livery stable.

When he got there he picked up the broom from its usual place and, holding it in his clumsy manner, attacked the floor with wide angry sweeps that left clear swaths through the dust and straw that lay there.

Orv Pickett looked in. "Say, Charlie, I said you didn't have to do that 'til tomorrow."

"I want to do it today," Charlie said through clenched teeth. "An' I'll fix that godamned door too."

By that evening Charlie had simmered down some. He sat on his bunk in the livery stable and waited for dusk when he would go over to Sly Webster's house for supper. After sweeping the floor and fixing the damaged door he had helped Orv Pickett lug some heavy team harnesses to a new storage area in the back of the barn. The leather implements were heavy and it pained his leg terribly to hobble under their weight, but the toil burned up the exces-

27

sive energy generated by the anger and frustration brought on by Ned Darwin.

The sun reddened into a deep crimson as it set before Charlie finally went outside and stumbled down the street toward Sly's. Despite the growing darkness he could see there were plenty of people on the street and he had no desire to meet anyone. He turned off the main thoroughfare and made his way down the alley that ran the length of the business district as he continued east.

When he arrived at Sly's back fence Charlie whistled softly to alert the Websters' dog Toby. The animal recognized him immediately and happily scampered up to be petted.

Toby followed as Charlie went around the side of the house toward the front porch. As he walked beneath the kitchen window he could hear Alma Webster's high-pitched voice raised in complaint.

"How come you keep invitin' him when I ask you not to?" she whined.

"Me an' Charlie's friends," Sly said. "Cain't I ask a friend over fer supper now and then?"

"The only reason you have anythin' to do with him at all is because he was a gunfighter hereabouts. You ain't got nothin' in common with him a'tall!"

"I like Charlie," Sly said. "And I enjoy listenin' to him tell me 'bout his adventures."

"An' lettin' him take them free baths ain't good business neither," she added emphatically.

"A little hot water don't cost much," Sly said.

"It does when he prob'ly keeps other folks away," she countered. "He's plumb awful lookin', Sly!"

"Now, he got shot up bad. Ever'body knows that."

"That don't change a thing 'bout the way he looks," Alma said. "Ugh! That awful ol' hand o' his

28

all curled up an' funny white-lookin' like that. Why don't he at least have the decency to put a glove on? I swear it's all I can do to eat when he's here."

Charlie reached down and gave Toby a parting pat, then limped through the back gate toward the livery stable as Alma's high-pitched, whining voice still echoed in his ears.

The end of a perfect day.

By the time he was back in his meager lodgings, Charlie didn't honestly know how he felt. He was drained and washed out, like a hollow nothingness that mattered not a whit to anyone or anything. A man has to be respected—not necessarily loved—but that esteem, no matter how slight, has to be a mighty important part of life.

Charlie tried to figure out what he had going for him. He was barely getting by. The only pleasures in his life were getting good and drunk once a month and eating his one supper a day. There was no question he would never go to Sly Webster's shop or house again. There was absolutely nothing positive in his life—it all added up to zero.

He made the awful decision in an instant.

It was like an instinctive quick-draw when the gun cleared leather in one unthinking flash of a second. But this time the muzzle wasn't aimed toward an opponent. It would fire into his own head, blowing out the brain that could no longer control part of a damaged body.

His pistol, along with the sawed off double-barrelled Greener shotgun, was still over at the marshal's office. Charlie had never seen the sense in picking them up. He had gone in there once when Nolan Edgewater was still in Wichita and had seen that they were being taken care of. The shotgun had even been used on a couple of occasions and that had been all right with Charlie too.

But now he would choose which one—the Colt or the Greener—would take him out of his misery.

The shotgun would blow his head clear off his shoulders. He really didn't care what his corpse looked like, but that would make a hell of a lot of gore for somebody to pick up. Even if he went out a ways in the country—he didn't want to make any messes for Orv Pickett in the livery stable—somebody would be required to bring his remains.

Charlie's final plans, once formed, were simple enough. He would treat himself to an orgy of eating until he'd used up all the meals he had coming in two days.

Then, on the second night, he would get his monthly whiskey on the cuff from O'Reilly the bartender, go out of town and get as drunk as he possibly could with deep, heavy drinking. After sobering up the next day, he'd do the job on himself.

Charlie could picture Sly Webster spending the rest of his life cutting hair and shaving faces while boring the hell out of everyone in Wichita with his tales of friendship with the legendary ex-Marshal Charlie Martell.

Charlie leaned back on his bunk and smiled to himself. He actually had to admit he was looking forward to the episode with the revelry of food and whiskey, and the final touch on the life of Charles Houston Martell: a self-inflicted .45 slug.

There was one sudden feeling of regret that gripped him. He remembered the Indian superstition that if a man was maimed during his time on earth, his sould would carry the inflictions into the afterlife. That was why they always mutilated dead enemies.

Lord above, Charlie thought, *don't let it be true!*

chapter 3

Molly, the girl at the railroad depot cafe, grinned at Charlie as he stamped through the door for the fourth time that day.

"You hongry again, Mister Martell?" she asked.

"Yes indeed, missy," Charlie said cheerfully. "Still got them beans and bacon?"

"They whupped up some cornbread since you was here last," the girl said. "I'll fetch you some directly." She went to the back of the little eatery and came back tailed by a whiskery old man wearing an indescribably filthy apron. He nodded politely to Charlie. "Howdy."

"Howdy," Charlie said.

"I jest wanted to see the feller that's been eatin' all my cookin'," the old man said. "You really like it that much?"

"Sure," Charlie said.

"Or maybe yo're a-eatin' it 'cause the city's payin', huh?"

"Oh, no," Charlie said. "It's that good. I'm celebrating a big happenin' in my life and cain't think of a better way to do it."

"Yo're a strange 'un," the cook said. "I've had cowpokes beat the shit outta me before after I served 'em outta my chuck wagon. I may have improved some from them days, but not that much."

Norb Preston, the cafe owner, came out and grabbed the cook by the shoulder and wordlessly shoved him back to work. He eyed Charlie carefully. "My reckonin' tells me this is yore last meal 'til tomorry."

"Mine too," Charlie said agreeably. Since he'd made his decision, he felt as if all the burdens in his life had disolved away.

"Well, since you started that ruckus over the number o' meals you git, I keep close tabs."

Not long after Charlie had been granted the meal ticket, he had missed a few times. Preston had refused to make them up to him, but later Charlie found the cafe owner had charged the city anyhow. Since Nolan Edgewater was still a marshal it had been an easy matter to make things right. From then on Charlie got everything due him, despite Preston's protests.

"You ain't still mad at me fer makin' you out a cheat, are you, Norb?"

Preston pointed a menacing finger at him. "You jest watch yoreself, Martell."

Charlie only grinned as Molly sat the plate in front of him. A generous slab of cornbread sat on top of the greasy repast, pale and undercooked on top, golden in the middle and burned black on the bottom. But Charlie didn't care. All he wanted was this one last chance to get the wrinkles out of his belly. A little later he would hit up the Palace Saloon for his whiskey, then head out for the country. By this time tomorrow, Charlie figured, his days of humiliation would be over.

As he ate, the northbound from Caldwell came steaming into the depot with loud hisses and a clanging bell. It squealed to a deafening stop as the noise engulfed the little cafe.

The engineer and fireman appeared at the counter after about ten minutes. They took a look at what Charlie was eating and settled for coffee.

"Sure you boys don't want nothin' to eat?" Preston asked.

"No, thanks," the engineer said. "How's things in Wichita?"

"Mighty quiet," Preston replied as he poured them each a cup. "I think the ol' place is settlin' down finally."

"Well, friend, things ain't settled down a bit down in Caldwell," the fireman joined in. "Had 'em one hell of a shootin' 'bout three days or so ago."

"Lots o' folks shot?" Preston asked.

"Nope. Jest a U.S. Marshal tryin' to make an arrest. But they was enough bullets flyin' to redo the Battle o' Gettysburg."

Charlie, interested, looked up. "Who was the lawman?"

"A feller used to be here name o' Edgewater," the engineer said.

"Nolan Edgewater?"

"Yep. You know him?"

Preston pointed at Charlie. "That's Charlie Martell. Him and Edgewater was marshals here in Wichita a few years back."

"I'll be damned!" the fireman marveled. "So yo're Charlie Martell?"

"Yeah. How's Edgewater?"

"Deader'n a goddammed quartered buffalo . . . I'm afraid," the eingineer interjected.

Charlie dropped his fork. "Just what in hell happened?"

The engineer sensed the sudden anger and stammered a little. "Well . . . he, uh, had . . . it seems that Edgewater was trailin' this feller name o' Dandy Kilgallen through the Injun territory. Had him a warrant from Judge Parker over to Fort Smith. Kilgallen went up north to Caldwell and Edgewater caught up with him there. When the marshal tried to arrest him, Kilgallen an' some of his friends shot him."

"Goddammit!" Charlie exclaimed as his face grew pale in anger. "What happened to this here Kilgallen?"

"Nothin'," the engineer said with a shrug.

"What do you mean nothin'? Did he ride out?"

The fireman shook his head. "Hell, he's better off in Caldwell than anywhere else. The marshal there's a old pard o' his. Leastways that's what I hear."

"Who's this marshal?" Charlie asked.

"Harry Green."

"That no good sonofabitch!" Charlie said under his breath. He got to his feet and limped out to the depot platform. Harry Green was an old nemesis of both his and Nolan Edgewater's. They had arrested him on robbery charges in Wichita which resulted in a conviction. Before that they knew him from Abilene and had seen a murder charge fade away when the resulting trial ended in a hung jury. The fact that Green was now a lawman wasn't too surprising. More than one sheriff or marshal had to avoid crossing a state line here and there.

Charlie shuffled down the street to the marshal's office. A young lawman sat at the desk idly reading the latest edition of the *Wichita Eagle.* He looked up and recognized Charlie. "Howdy, Mister Martell."

36

"Howdy. Y'all hear 'bout Nolan Edgewater?"

"Got hisself shot over at Caldwell," the youngster said matter-of-factly.

"How come nobody tole me 'bout it?"

The kid shrugged. "I don't know."

"I want my shotgun and Peacemaker—the belt and holster too."

"Sure, Mister Martell." He walked to the wallrack and retrieved the double-barrelled weapon, then handed it to Charlie. "I think there's some shells that belong to it in the desk drawer."

"I'll take 'em."

"Here's the Colt too."

Charlie clumsily held on to the items as he turned toward the door. The kid frowned in confusion. "What do you want them things for? You ain't goin' to Caldwell, are you? Hell, there ain't nothin' you can do over there, Mister Martell."

Charlie stopped in the door, deep in thought for several seconds, then looked back at the kid. "You better git me my old set o' handcuffs and leg irons too."

The young lawman fetched them from a bottom desk drawer. "Christ! You must figger there's *somethin'* you might accomplish."

Charlie didn't acknowledge the remarks. Instead he went straight back to his room at the livery stable and dumped the weapons on the bunk. Then he sat down trying to sort things out in his head. But there was already one thing clearly decided:

Nolan Edgewater's death would not go unavenged.

The next morning was marked by Orv Pickett's voice exploding across the livery yard like the report of a Winchester carbine. "*Goddammit, Charlie!* What the hell do you mean you want to borry a horse? Hell, I don't make my livin' *loanin'* 'em out, I *rent* 'em out!"

Charlie stood there calmly in his clumsy way and kept his voice at a reasonable level. "I feel awful askin' you, Orv, I really do. And I wouldn't if it weren't important."

"Cain't somebody else bury that dead friend o' yor'n over at Caldwell?"

"I got to see to the arrangements," Charlie lied. "Besides I don't need one o'yore best animals."

"Well, thank the Lord fer that!" Orve interrupted.

". . . I just need one that's carry me there an' back."

Orv shook his head in disbelief. "Charlie, you do take the cake."

"Hell, I got my own saddle," Charlie said.

"Shit! You ain't tended to that thing in five years," Orv said.

"I looked her over last night," Charlie said. "She's a little dried and cracked here and there, but she'll do the job. Got my own bridle, too."

Orv finally gave in. "Jesus, I must be loco. Help yoreself to the old gray then. An' don't you tarry none, you hear?"

"I won't," Charlie said, clumping back toward the livery barn. "Soon as I finish my business there I'll be back." He didn't expect to be back at all, but even if Orv lost the old horse, it wouldn't be much of a setback to his business.

He went to the horse's stall and led the elderly animal outside to the door of his room. Then he went inside and returned with the bridle "Easy," Charlie said as he slid the crown piece of the leather arrangement over the horse's head and settled it in place. "Good ol' feller," he said as he gently stuck his thumb in the brute's mouth to make him open up for the bit. He inserted it carefully as he drew the ears under the crown piece and arranged the forelock. After securing the throat latch he returned to his room for the saddle.

Within twenty minutes the animal was ready for the trip. Charlie's meager amount of gear was rolled up in a rather scrawny bedroll and tied on. After slipping the shotgun into its boot he was ready to go.

"When you figger on bein' back?" Orv asked with a worried tone as he walked up to him.

"Soon," Charlie said.

"Hey! How come yo're wearin' yore iron . . . and carryin' that damn scattergun o' yor'n?"

"Pertection," Charlie said. "You know how wild Caldwell is." He slipped his left foot into the stirrup and grimaced unintentionally as his full weight was taken up by his bad right leg. Then he pulled himself up into the saddle. His stiff limb stuck out at an awkward angle.

"Damn, if'n you ain't a sight," Orv said. "You cain't even git yore damn leg into the other stirrup. Wait a minute while I let 'er out fer ya." He adjusted the arrangement, then slipped Charlie's boot into position. "There you go, pard. Have a nice ride."

"Thank you kindly," Charlie said. He flicked the reins and rode out of the livery yard to turn south toward the open prairie.

"Remember you said you'd be back soon," Orv called.

Charlie waved his agreement.

"An somethin' else, goddammit! They hang hossthieves!"

* * *

Caldwell, south of Wichita, was at the terminus of the Southern Central and Fort Scott Railway. It had existed with a little under three hundred people until the railroad showed up in 1879. Then the population shot up to 1,500 and the place became known as "The Border Queen" in relation to its location on the Indian Territory line. It was boisterous and booming as tough frontier types and cowboys crowded over its city limits to create one of the wildest towns in the west.

Charlie, because of his physical problems, took it easy on his trip and made use of frequent rest stops to ease the pain in his bad leg. Still, there was no hurry so he had no feeling of impatience as he set up a cold camp that night. There was no sense in a fire. The weather was too good for one and he didn't have as much as a pot of coffee to heat up—or a cigar to light. He lay there with his head on his saddle and the blanket beneath him and stared up at the stars.

The sky in Kansas on a clear night is a black far-reaching dome that stretches widely from flat horizon to horizon in a huge panorama of blinking stars. Its hugeness is enough to shrink a man's ego when he realizes what an insignificant little thing he really is. But Charlie's mind wasn't on philosophical thoughts. He concentrated on his friend Nolan Edgewater.

Nolan was a North Carolinian who had come west. He, too, was a Confederate veteran without much at home. They met while serving as law officers in Abilene and the sharing of dangers and unpleasant duties while backing each other to the hilt—while proving each's dependability to the other—forged a p, lasting friendship.

40

But Nolan couldn't get along with Marshal Hickok at all and soon left for Wichita. After Charlie's troubles with the drovers over the stolen herd, he figured he might as well head south and join him.

Serving the law with Nolan Edgewater had been a genuine pleasure. Nolan was a short, sandy-haired fellow with a well-kept mustache. Blue eyed, with a pleasant sort of smile, he was as brave as they came. Sometimes, especially when facing down a saloonful of crazed, drunken cowboys, Charlie would recharge his flagging courage with a glance at Nolan's steady gaze and determined attitude, knowing the two of them were unbeatable. And he had probably been right. Charlie had been crippled when Nolan wasn't around—that is, until the last minute when he'd taken on the two bank robbers and save Charlie's life—and Nolan had been shot to death without Charlie there to back him up.

Charlie sighed and felt the loneliness overtake his emotions. He would be joining Nolan soon, if there was a life after death, and he didn't regret it a bit. But now, by God, there were a couple of other sons of bitches going to greet the devil with them.

chapter 4

By the time Charlie reached the outskirts of Caldwell a bit after dawn, he was ravenous. He had no food with him and not a cent to purchase any. As he slowly rode among the first outhouses and chicken yards behind the outlying domiciles he spotted a large two-story dwelling. There was a woman in the back chopping kindling. Charlie pulled on the reins and let the horse amble up to her picket fence.

"Mornin', Ma'am."

She turned around and looked at him. "Good mornin'."

"I'd be proud to chop that kindlin' fer my breakfast, if you please."

She looked pointedly at him and hesitated before speaking. "Well . . . I suppose. Please come in and get started if you want to."

Charlie shrugged his bad leg out of the stirrup and swung from the saddle to the ground. He felt self-conscious as he scuffled through the gate and walked up to her. He stopped and removed his hat. "Charlie Martell at yore service, Ma'am."

"How do you do, Mister Martell. I'm Mrs. Koch. If you want, I'll give you breakfast fer the kindlin'."

"Yes, Ma'am." Charlie reached out with his good hand and took the ax from her.

She was a skinny woman appearing to be in her mid-thirties. Her auburn-colored hair was lifeless as if hurriedly arranged in a convenient manner that took little time. She was freckled, with a small hawkish nose and a thin mouth that seemed without humor. She looked pointedly at Charlie. "Are you sure yo're up to this?"

"All it takes is one good hand, Ma'am," Charlie said. "I handle this chore 'bout ever'day over in Wichita where I live."

She nodded a reluctant agreement. "As long as you can do it then. I run a boarding house here and me an' my hired girl are tryin' to cook up breakfast. It'll help some if you hurry up."

"Yes, Ma'am." Charlie, who had developed a pretty fair method of handling kindling at the livery stable, set to work in his own style. He set the wood on end on the chopping block (in this case the stump of a tree) and drove the ax into the top. Then the whole affair was lifted up and smartly struck down on the stump, slipping the wood. He looked up at her on the back porch. "See?"

She nodded her approval and went inside as Charlie set to work. Routine tasks requiring little concentration were pleasant for him. He let his mind dwell on the deadly job ahead of him that day as he performed his chore in an efficient, rhythmic way. The ax rose and fell in a syncopated chop, chop, as the kindling pile grew by the back door.

Presently Mrs. Koch came out and looked at the wood pile. "I reckon you know yore business," she said. "But come on inside now. We're servin' breakfast."

"I don't think I done enough to earn my grub, Mrs. Koch."

44

"O'course you ain't! But I'm sure you don't want yore breakfast to git cold. You eat now and finish yore work later."

"Yes, Ma'am. Thank you kindly." He set the ax down and followed her into the kitchen. He could see her boarders through a serving window. They sat at a large round table in the main dining room. His own meal was on the kitchen table. He was pleasantly surprised as he sat down. There were three eggs, a generous pile of bacon, biscuits and a smear of honey on his plate. Beside it sat a large mug of hot coffee. As he ate, Mrs. Koch and her hired girl rushed in and out of the door taking care of the boarders. Charlie was surprised that such a skinny woman could display so much energy and physical strength as she carried heavy pitchers and trays of plates out to what seemed about a half dozen hungry men.

He glanced at her as she came back for more. "Them fellers seem to eat a lot."

"Most of 'em's railroad men," Mrs. Koch explained. "Hard workers like that need lots o' food."

"I reckon," he said agreeably as he wiped up his egg yolk with a biscuit. "Yo're a mighty generous person." He stood up. "Well, I'm gonna git back to the kindlin' then."

"Fine, Mister Martell," she said picking up a pot of coffee from the stove. "I'll be out to check yore work in a bit."

Charlie felt an instant stab of resentment. He didn't like womenfolk checking anything he did. But he was grateful for the big meal. "Yes, Ma'am."

Charlie went back to work. Within an hour the woodbin was filled and he decided enough was enough. He knocked on the kitchen door and Mrs. Koch appeared there. Her hands were wet and

45

soapy. "Yes, Mister Martell?"

"I'm finished, ma'am. Where's you like me to put the ax?"

"Hang it on them two nails there," she said pointin' to a place on the wall. "Then I'll have another chore for you."

"Another chore?" Charlie asked. "I figgered I was finished."

"Hardly," she said sternly. "I have to do my shoppin' an' I'll need someone to tote the heavier things."

"Beggin' your pardon, ma'am, but I got business here in Caldwell today. I asked fer breakfast in exchange fer choppin' kindlin'. I took care o' all you had, so I reckon we're quits."

"Well, we ain't!" she said emphatically, that thin mouth drawn tight. "As you can well see I need to git another load o' wood and I cain't handle that myself. Neither can my helpin' girl.'

"Ma'am . . ."

"Didn't you like your breakfast, Mister Martell?"

"Yes I did. It was plumb fillin', Mrs. Koch, but . . ."

"You can come in for a cup o' coffee if you want. Then we'll go into town."

Charlie, who dearly wanted a cup of coffee, hesitated nevertheless as he looked pointedly at her wet hands. "I ain't washin' dishes."

"An' nobody expects you to," Mrs. Koch said.

Charlie went back to the kitchen table and was served another generous mug of the hot brew.

"I see you hurt yoreself bad," Mrs. Koch said.

"I reckon it's pretty obvious," Charlie said between sips of coffee.

"I got to tell you, mister," the thin woman said, "I

46

ain't never seen a body so banged up and still movin' around. Unless it were bullets that maimed you."

"I was a lawman in Wichita," Charlie said, annoyed. "Let's just say I come off second best."

"We had a gunfight here a few days back," she said as she continued her attack on the dirty dishes. "A United States marshal got hisself killed."

"Men die ever'day," Charlie said. He didn't want her to know he was at all interested in the event. Long experience taught him the fewer people that know about a showdown, the less complicated the affair becomes.

"I lost my husband right after we moved here from Missouri," Mrs. Koch said. "Died o' consumption or somethin'. Never did call a doctor—he didn't trust 'em—so he got sicker an' sicker until he slipped away."

As she continued to talk, Charlie decided to shrug off the situation he had gotten into here. While she was shopping he could call on the marshal and get into the real business ahead of him. He suddenly had the thought that this stoney lady might have to tote her goods home alone.

Matilda Koch drove her buckboard into the business district as Charlie rode his horse beside the conveyance. The woman wore a small-brimmed, flowered straw hat tied under her chin with a broad red ribbon. A tasseled shaw, gaudy with a woven peacock design on it, was draped across her shoulders, and a yellow shopping basket sat beside her on the seat.

"I'll be needin' you in about a hour," she said, pulling up in front of the general store. "From here we'll go to the wood yard and then to the livery. I

47

need oats." She gave a sympathetic look to the old horse Charlie was riding. "I think we'll give some to that pore animal yo're tormentin'. When's the last time you gave him a good feed?" She didn't wait for an answer as she climbed down from the vehicle. She started to walk off, but hesitated and came back. "Don't you start drinkin', hear?" She gave Charlie's mount one more sympathetic look. "Shame about that horse."

"He ain't mine," Charlie said sullenly. "I . . . I rented him from the livery in Wichita."

"No excuse fer mistreatin' a horse, Mister Martell," Matty Koch said. "An' don't you fergit . . . be here in an hour!"

"Damn!"

"What?"

"I said, 'Yes, Ma'am,' " Charlie said. He watched her march her boney frame up the front steps of the store, then he urged his horse down the street where a faded wooden sign announced the location of the marshal. He hitched his horse at a rail twenty feet from the jailhouse door. Then, with the shotgun across his shoulder, he warily hobbled toward his destination, keeping an eye on the street.

His caution, wise as it was, was unnecessary. There was only one man in the office and Charlie recognized him instantly. "Howdy, Harry."

Marshal Harry Green looked up, startled, then his face relaxed into an easy grin. "I'll be damned! Charlie Martell of all people." He watched him carefully as the ex-lawman approached his desk. "Damn! You did git crippled up some, didn't you?"

"I reckon," Charlie said. "Know why I'm here?"

Green smiled. "Yeah, I got a idee."

"How come you didn't arrest Kilgallen after he

48

shot Nolan?"

"He escaped," Green said.

"Yo're a damn liar!"

Green's mouth twitched in anger but he carefully eyed the shotgun. "Mebbe I oughta throw you in jail fer disturbin' the peace."

Charlie ignored the threat. "Where's Kilgallen?"

Green smiled again and leaned back in his chair. "You gonna call him out, Charlie?"

"There's a warrant fer him. Got a copy?"

"Sure. I got Edgewater's. Took it off his body," Green said. "You figurin' on servin' it?"

"Might as well."

"You ain't a lawman no more, are you?"

"Call it a citizen's arrest," Charlie said.

Green guffawed and reached in his desk drawer, withdrawing an official document. He shoved it across to Charlie. "You'll find Dandy down at the Exchange Saloon. Go on along and do yore duty—I'll come by in about fifteen minutes or so . . . to carry you down to the undertaker's."

Charlie took the warrant and carefully backed out of the office. When he was sure Green wouldn't come after him, he turned and stamped down the street to the saloon. He paused at the batwings and sized up the room.

There were three men being served at the bar while another sat at a table playing solitaire. The card player was obviously no gunhawk—except, perhaps, for the hidden weapon to protect himself from an unruly loser—but the other three were rough characters, which meant they might be friends of Dandy Kilgallen, who was among those at the bar.

Charlie swallowed hard as normal fears and apprehensions made themselves plainly noticeable. He

49

realized that within the next fifteen seconds he could be lying out on the saloon floor as dead as Nolan Edgewater had been. He took a deep breath and let it out slowly, then he stepped in and leveled the shotgun, holding his crippled arm under it for support.

"Dandy Kilgallen!"

The gambler leaped from the table and backed up with both hands showing plain. The men at the bar turned, then two of them stepped rapidly away as the bartender sank out of sight. The third drinker turned nonchalantly and eyed Charlie carefully. Then he straightened up, alarmed when he noted Charlie's weapon. "Easy does it, pard," he said. Then he recognized his challenger. "Hell's fire! If it ain't ol' Charlie Martell—all crippled up and big as life. How you doin', Charlie?"

Charlie ignored the question. "I got a warrant fer yore arrest issured from the federal court at Fort Smith, Arkansas. I'm also takin' you in fer the murder of Nolan Edgewater."

"I didn't shoot nobody," Kilgallen said.

"Drop yore gunbelt with yore left hand," Charlie said as he ignored the obvious lie and edged toward Kilgallen with his awkward shuffle.

"Shit!" Kilgallen exclaimed. "There ain't no crippled sonofabitch takin' me nowhere." He made his play so quick that Charlie's rusty instincts made him squeeze both triggers without thinking.

The shotgun bucked and flew up to hit him in the shoulder, knocking him to the floor. The blast went wide with only a portion of the shot hitting Kilgallen's left arm. The outlaw spun around and slammed against the bar.

Charlie was on his back, frantically recalling the day he was crippled, as he clawed for his pistol with his left hand. Kilgallen recovered somewhat and aimed dizzily at Charlie, who rolled away from the shot. By then Charlie had the Colt out and squeezed the trigger twice without aiming as he worked his left hand clumsily.

Both shots went wide.

Kilgallen quickly regained his equilibrium and was ready to kill. "They'll bury that damn warrant with you," he hissed.

Charlie tried to aim again as instinctively his crippled hand flew up to the pistol and pressed hard on the trigger guard for a better hold. Surprisingly, the weapon was stable and he found himself looking down the sights on a steady barrel. He squeezed the trigger and instantly Kilgallen leaped back under the force of the slug's impact. Somehow he managed to keep to his feet as Charlie nearly rejoiced in the shooting procedure he had accidentally discovered. One more quick but unwavering shot whipped the fugitive to the floor like he'd been struck by some giant's pick handle.

The room was suddenly quite as everyone's ears rang from the explosions that had rocked the place for a short time. Charlie got unsteadily to his feet and stood at the bar. Kilgallen was sprawled out ten feet from him. He stamped over and inspected the body carefully, then turned a mean eye toward the others in the room.

"It was a fair fight," the gambler said taking the hint.

"Yes, sir," one of the other men said cautiously.

The bartender came up and nodded his own agreement with fearful enthusiasm.

Charlie felt good—damned good.

For the first time in five years people looked at

him with the old respect. He turned toward the door and saw several citizens peering in. Among them was an open-mouthed Matilda Koch. Charlie started to say something to her when Marshal Green pushed through the crowd, then stopped in unabashed wonder at the sight of Charlie standing there.

"Marshal, I come here to serve this warrant on that feller there," Charlie said loudly as he kept the legal aspects of the situation in mind. "He resisted arrest and I shot him dead. I got witnesses."

Green looked around at the others who nodded affirmatively. He sighed loudly, his agitation badly disguised. "Well, then! I reckon you better come on down to the jail with me, Charlie. I got to fill out a report on that warrant."

"By God, you'll do somethin' accordin' to the law after all," Charlie said, grinning. "And I got a few questions fer you while we're there."

Green motioned him to follow and started back for the jail. As Charlie stepped out of the saloon he nodded to Matilda Koch. "I'll be with you directly, Ma'am."

She raised her eyebrows slightly. "I'll wait at the buggy Mister Martell."

Green was waiting at the door when Charlie arrived. He slammed it shut as a sign to the crowd to keep away. As he pulled the necessary forms from his desk his face was red with anger. "You were one lucky sonofabitch."

"Easy, Harry, or I'll deal you some o' the same," Charlie said coldly.

"Not with me as marshal you won't!" Green said.

"I don't give a damn about you, Harry," Charlie said. "But I want to know who else was in on killin' Nolan. I know Kilgallen didn't do it alone."

52

Green looked up surprised. "You goin' after 'em all? Hell, you'll never make it through all of 'em, Charlie. You was just lucky with Dandy, that's it, plain and simple."

"You worried about me, Harry?"

"*God damn you!* If I could get away with it I'd shoot you myself. I owe you, Charlie," Green said. "Just like I owed Nolan Edgewater."

"Who else was in on the killin'?" Charlie asked. "I promise I'll go after 'em. That way mebbe you won't have to shoot me."

"All right, by God!" Green said as he leaned forward. "The others was fellers you know. John Dougherty and Cimarron Gleason."

Charlie's memory was triggered by the names. Dougherty was a vicious man who viewed the world as his for the taking. His reaction to resistance or denial by man, woman or child was instantaneous and violent. Cimarron Gleason was more of an adventurer who liked a challenge, but that didn't mean he wouldn't take advantage of any edge he could develop.

"Where they at?" Charlie asked.

"I don't know where Dougherty is, but Gleason is down in the Creek Nation at Muskogee. You can stop off there on yore way to Fort Smith."

"Why would I go to Fort Smith?" Charlie asked.

"There's a five hunnerd dollar reward on Dandy issued outta Judge Parker's court. All you gotta do is take this here report, and the death certificate the county coroner will issue, and cash 'em in!"

Five hundred dollars!

After the deprivations of the previous five years, that amount seemed a fortune to Charlie. He looked at Green. "How about Gleason and Dougherty? Any

53

reward money out on them?"

"Yo're a right greedy cuss, ain't you?" Green remarked. "But I'm sorry to tell you that I don't know of any. But if yo're thinkin' of goin' down to Muskogee yo're even crazier than fer comin' here to Caldwell. There ain't no marshal in his right mind that'd try an arrest in that hellhole."

"Mebbe I ain't in my right mind," Charlie said. "But I appreciate yore concern, Harry."

Green grinned. "Gleason is wanted over at Fort Smith concernin' a train robbery and murder. I thought you might like to know that in case yo're thinkin' o' gittin' yore revenge on him legal and square by deliverin' him there. Or do you figger on gunnin' him down in the Injun country?"

"I might just surprise the hell outta you and haul him over to that judge at Fort Smith. An' while I'm there I'll check to see if they want you fer somethin' too," Charlie said when the report Green was working on was finished. He picked it up and limped to the door. "I'll be back in a coupla days fer that death certificate."

"Don't rush," Green said. "It's nice havin' you around."

"Oh, you won't miss me long," Charlie said. "As soon as I'm finished with Gleason I'll be back fer you—man to man."

Green laughed. "Once you've crossed that state line you'll never be seen alive in Kansas again, Charlie!"

chapter 5

Life suddenly blossomed like a prairie flower after a spring rain for Charlie Martell. With Mrs. Koch's help he was able to turn in the authorization for the five hundred dollar reward to the local bank. The only stipulation was that he not draw more than a hundred of it until the balance came through from Fort Smith, Arkansas. But that inconvenience was solved when Matilda Koch generously co-signed herself into responsibility for the full amount.

That evening Charlie relaxed in the Koch parlor. He was now a bona fide paid-up boarder in the residence and was no longer required to run errands for his meals. This unexpected arrangement had been suggested by the landlady herself when they returned from the shopping trip.

"You look like you need a rest," Matty Koch had told him as he unloaded the firewood and oats after carrying in the groceries.

"I got things to do, ma'am," Charlie had protested. "What happened a while ago was just the first step in a job I got to finish."

Matty clucked her irritation and disagreement. "I'm gonna tell you straight out, Mister Martell, that yo're one o' the poorest fed specimens o' manhood I seen in a long time. I don't know where yo're gonna git the energy to catch them other two fellers you tole me about."

Charlie gave her comments more than a passing thought. What she said rang truer to life than he wanted to admit. For the past five years he had drunk hard and eaten poorly. He was not in the best physical condition because of it. Even a couple of weeks of abstinence and good solid food three times a day—along with some practice shooting—certainly wouldn't hinder him in his efforts. A gunman with a game arm and leg needed all the edge he could get. Besides, there were a couple of ideas he wanted to try out before he rode down into the Creek Nation after Cimarron Gleason.

The other boarders accepted him into their group with genuine pleasure. Two of the railroad workers had heard of him and were impressed even more now because of that day's work under his handicap.

"Weren't you askeered, Mister Martell?" one asked pointedly.

Another popped up quickly. "Hell, no, Marshal Charlie Martell never backed down from no man. Right, Mister Martell?"

Charlie smiled modestly. His belly was filled with fried chicken, baked potatoes, greens, biscuits and two large pieces of deep-dish apple pie. "I got to tell you boys the truth," he said. "Ever'time you go into a gunfight yore belly is tied up in knots. It's been awhile fer me today, and I was skitterish."

"Damn! That musta been some shootout today," the first speaker marveled. "They say that Dandy Kilgallen is as fast as fast can be."

"Ain't no pistolero gonna best a shotgun," Charlie said. "Even before I got hurt I preferred that Greener 12-gauge o' mine to whippin' out a handgun."

"Yo're the professional, so I cain't argue none with you," the other railroader said respectfully.

Another boarder, a printer on the Caldwell *Post* named Ned Orson, had been watching and listening silently all evening. Finally he spoke up. "Mister Martell, would you consent to an interview by my newspaper?"

"You mean somebody askin' me questions then writin' up my answers?" Charlie asked.

"Certainly," Orson said. "I could interview you and set the type myself. I promise to make you sound real good."

"You'll have to let me think on that," Charlie said.

Matilda Koch listened to the conversation with a great deal of interest. She rarely joined her boarders in the parlor in the evenings. She generally had too much work to do or thought it best to leave the men to their own brand of conversation as well as their cigars. But tonight was different. She was fascinated by this crippled stranger who had suddenly shown up from nowhere on her doorstep. Despite his punished body and the look in his eyes, she had sensed a tormented soul that was performing well below its capacity. She sat across the room from Charlie and knitted in silence at a contrived project that really meant nothing to her as she listened to the ex-marshal with more than just a passing interest. Now and then she patted her hair self-consciously. She had brushed it carefully just prior to supper and, before coming down to the parlor to visit, had arranged it once again.

"Would y'all like some coffee?" she said, finally interrupting.

"Yes, Ma'am," Charlie said. "That sounds mighty good to me."

"You don't mind if we put a little somethin' extry in it, do you, Mrs. Koch?" one of the railroaders asked, patting the pint bottle in his vest.

"Not fer me, thanks," Charlie said as he held out his hand that shook a trifle. "I got to steady down some. There's one hell of a job—pardon, Mrs. Koch—waitin' fer me in the next coupla weeks or so."

On her way to the kitchen, Matilda Koch paused in the doorway to give Charlie Martell a look of appoval and respect.

Charlie was keenly aware of the stares directed at him as he limped down the street to the gunsmith's carrying his shotgun. But this time it was like the old days. He held his head high and avoided no eyeball-to-eyeball contact with passing strangers. His success of two days before brought to mind a danger he had not considered in a long time: the punk kid out to make a reputation or prove himself by gunning down a known fighter. The fact that he was crippled meant little now that Dandy Kilgallen had been laid to rest with shotgun pellets and two slugs from Charlie Martell's personal arsenal in him.

The gunsmith looked up in undisguised curiosity as Charlie shuffled into his shop. "Can I help you, Mister Martell?" The accent was Minnesota Swede.

"Yeah," Charlie said. "I got a couple o' things to take care of. First thing I need is a left-handed holster and rig. Got one?"

"Yes, sir. I have three you can choose from." He brought up the items from under the counter and spread them out for Charlie's close inspection. Then he offered his hand. "Gus Swensen."

58

Charlie shook it awkwardly with his left as he introduced himself.

"Oh, yeah, I know who you are. Everybody in Caldwell is talking about you."

Charlie slid his pistol in and out of the merchandise before choosing one. "Not too loose and not too tight," he said almost to himself. "I don't expect to be fast with the thing, but I don't want a hang-up there either."

"All of 'em are in pretty good shape," Swensen said.

"Do you do your own leatherwork?" Charlie asked.

"No, sir. There's a bootmaker—Tom Linker—down the street. He can make any adjustments you want."

"I don't want nothin' done to the holster," Charlie said. "I got somethin' else in mind." He put the shotgun on the counter. "How 'bout takin' three inches off this stock."

Swensen winced. "By golly, that scroll work there is sure pretty to be running a saw through it."

"Perty don't git you shit in what I'm usin' it fer," Charlie said. "It's three inches longer'n I want it."

"I'll saw it off for nothing," Swensen said painfully. "But I hate to ruin good workmanship."

"Ruin it," Charlie said without sentimentality.

The gunsmith measured off three inches after locking the weapon in his bench vise. He gave Charlie one more imploring look then regretfully did as he had been told. He brought the altered gun back. "Here you go, Mister Martell. That was a real shame."

"Some things cain't be helped," Charlie said as he left the shop carrying both the shotgun and the new holster. Within minutes he was in the bootmaker's placing his order. "I want a good, stuffed pad made up fer the butt o' this stock here."

Linker, the leather craftsman, gave the matter a few moments of thought. "I take it that this is fer the recoil."

"Right," Charlie said. "I don't want my arm beat black and blue ever' time I fire this thing."

"I think I can make somethin' you can lace up," Linker said. "That way you can slip it on or off as it pleases you."

"It's got to be good and steady—it ain't ever comin' off."

"I'll mount it up with tacks an' brass studs then," Linker said. "She'll never come off 'less'n you pull 'em out."

"Good," Charlie said. "How soon can I have it?"

"Three days . . . mebbe four or five."

"Take yore time an' make it good," Charlie said. "It's important to me."

"Don't you worry, Mister Martell," Linker said.

"I'll check in from time to time 'til the job's finished," Charlie said.

Linker scratched his head. "I figger you ain't gonna be shootin' this shotgun in the usual manner. But I'll be damned if'n I can figger out why."

"It gives me the edge on polecats," Charlie said as he left the shop.

A week later Charlie had ridden a ways out of town. He dismounted and hobbled the horse before he clumped out some fifty feet with a bag he carried with him. This held some empty bottles that he tied to the low branches of a cottonwood that grew on a creek bank.

After arranging the bottles the way he wanted he

60

returned to the horse and got his saddlebags, the shotgun and an old blanket he had borrowed from Mrs. Koch. He lay the blanket on the ground and inspected the new, heavy leather padding that was mounted on the butt of the weapon. He patted it heavily with a feeling of satisfaction.

Finally he was ready. He lay the shotgun across his good arm, sideways so that it pointed out barrel-over-barrel. He pulled it in as tight as he could to his bicep and tested how steady he could hold it. When he was finally satisfied, he aimed as best he could at one of the bottles and fired. The glass shattered as the pad took up the bite of the recoil. Then he immediately dropped the weapon to the old blanket at his feet. This simulated a barroom floor and the covering kept the dirt from getting into the barrels or mechanism. Then he drew his pistol with his left hand and brought the crippled right one up to steady it as he had done in the gunfight with Dandy Kilgallen. He squeezed the trigger—and missed.

Undaunted, he loaded the shotgun again and repeated the procedure. Both barrels on the weapon belched smoke and pellets. Then, after dropping it, he went to the pistol and took a little longer to aim this time. The bottle he had chosen exploded as the bullet tore through it.

Charlie smiled and went back to practicing.

This procedure became one he followed twice daily as he perfected his technique. It was too difficult to handle each trigger on the shotgun seperately so he decided to go in with both barrels at first opportunity. This had worried him at first but as his proficiency with the pistol increased, he felt more confident. But, still, he had to admit he was facing an uphill battle. If his opponent survived the prelimi-

61

nary fusillade as Kilgallen had done, he stood little chance of having time to use the pistol anyway. He couldn't expect to continue to be lucky, but the pistol's slim second chance was better than none at all—maybe.

But even after hours of practice he would slip now and then, leaving the bottle to swing unscathed in the breeze. Then the old feelings of incompetence and uselessness would return to batter down his emotions, but somehow he managed to fight back and recover enough to go on again. After all, he had seriously planned suicide, so even if, or when, Cimarron Gleason or John Dougherty killed him, it would be more useful and satisfying to die attempting to avenge Nolan Edgewater than by blowing out his brains himself.

It was still dark as Charlie stood at his room's window and looked out over the blackness of the prairie's expanse. He had been in Caldwell almost a month now. He was well fed and rested, his physical conditioning about as peak as it could be from so much clean living. His shooting techniques and abilities were developed to their utmost as well. Perhaps not in a superlative manner, but Charlie never had been that fast or that good a shot. He depended on coolness and quick thinking, two attributes he would need doubly now.

He turned from the window and began to methodically dress. The early morning chill caused his hurts to act up some, but he ignored the discomfort. Mrs. Koch had a bathtub he used daily. Although it wasn't as big as the one at Sly Webster's in Wichita, he worked out a way to use it to his advantage. He knew he would miss it.

After a last look around the room to make sure he had forgotten nothing—particularly any of the new clothes he had purchased with the reward money—he slipped on the gunbelt, grabbed the altered shotgun and saddlebags, then tiptoed silently down the hall to the stairs. Surprisingly, there was a light in the kitchen.

"Good mornin', Mister Martell," Matty Koch said from the doorway. "Like some breakfast before you leave?"

Charlie stood at the foot of the steps. "Yes, Ma'am. Thank you kindly, I didn't expect nobody to be up this time o' day."

Matty shrugged her skinny shoulders. "It's only a hour earlier'n usual fer me. So I thought I'd see you off with a full belly."

"I'm obliged," Charlie said sincerely. He went into the warm kitchen and sat down at the table. She served him some scrambled eggs and a huge cut of steak. As he dove in with gusto she returned to the stove to get a pan of hot biscuits.

"No butter," she said apologetically. "What I had turned rancid on me. Got to git the hired girl to churn up another batch. How about strawberry jam or honey?"

"I'm particular fond o' honey on my biscuits, if you please, Mrs. Koch," Charlie said.

"O'course I remember how you like coffee in the mornin'," she said. "Got a big pot boilin' now . . . fresh grounds, too."

"My belly's gonna think I died and went to heaven," Charlie said with his slight grin.

"Yo're just sayin' that now," Matty said, pouring him a mugful of the dark, strong liquid. She sat down on the other side of the table. "What're you gonna do after you git that jasper yo're after?"

"Come back up here to Caldwell and pester Marshal Green 'til I git a bead on the other feller I'm lookin' fer."

"Mister Martell, what . . . er, do you think you can handle 'em all right? I mean . . . well, that some o' the men around here been sayin' you got a disadvantage."

"I know I do," Charlie conceded. "But it's somethin' I got to take care of. That feller they shot here was my best friend. I cain't just let it slip by." He didn't mention the miserable life that was his alternative to death. He fully expected to catch lead from one of his quarries, and that would solve everything . . . honor and escape.

Matty smiled weakly. "You just do yore best an' the good Lord'll look after you. He favors sober men."

"Well, I'm havin' to stay sober—that's a fact," Charlie said. "By the way, I writ out a piece o' paper an' left it up there in my room. It's kinda hard to read 'cause I had to do it left handed, but it says that in case o' my death any money I got comin' fom any rewards or left over from the Kilgallen bounty be split between you and Mrs. Nolan Edgewater. She's the widder o' the friend I'm avengin'."

"You shouldn't'a done that, Mister Martell. I ain't kin to you or nothin'," Matty said.

"I just want to repay you fer the kindnesses you showed me here in the past weeks."

Matty, her eyes shining, gave him a fond look. "I'll put you in my prayers, Mister Martell. I think what yo're doin' is a noble thing and I admire you greatly fer it."

Charlie, puzzled by this show of respect, finished

64

his meal as she hovered over him with offers of second servings as well as flattering words. Her smile seemed genuine as she accompanied him to the back porch.

He looked up at her from the bottom of the steps. "Goodby, Mrs. Koch. Thank you again."

"Yo're surely welcome, Mister Martell," she said with a quaver in her voice. As he went through the front gate she called out again. "I'll have yore room waitin' fer you when you come back from the Injun country."

"Thank you," Charlie said.

"You be careful, you hear?"

"Yes, ma'am."

"I'll pray fer you, Mister Martell. Don't you fergit that!"

chapter 6

Muskogee, in the Creek Nation of the Indian Territory, was a hodgepodge of tents, crude frame buildings and tumble-down shacks. The location of the settlement was at the end of the Missouri, Kansas and Texas Railroad line into that area. The idea behind it was to supply a shipping point for the cattle drives up from Texas and, like all new towns that made sudden appearances along the rails, this one was a bad place inhabited by some of the meanest and toughest elements of the sparse frontier population.

In that land, destined to become the state of Oklahoma, were located the Five Civilized Tribes—the Cherokee, Creek, Choctaw, Chickasaw and Seminole Indians—as directed in the 1830's by the United States government. They lived in this large area under their own tribal laws and customs which were enforced by the Indian police known as the Lighthorse. These people administered their own courts and systems of justice although they had no jurisdiction over whites or other Indians who committed crimes against or with whites. During the Civil War these slave-holding Native Americans sided with the Confederacy and in 1866 were punished for serving the losing side by being forced to give up the western half of their lands to the wild Plains Indians. Since that time the Indian Territory became the haven, headquarters and abode of countless outlaws who hid in the wild and isolated areas, practically daring U.S. marshals to search them out and deliver them to justice at the federal court in Fort Smith, Arkansas.

Charlie rode into Muskogee with his shotgun across his lap. His position in the saddle with the right leg sticking out caused a few curious stares, but not much else. The people that moved about in the area were a mixture of Indians, blacks and a few rough looking white men. Somewhere in that hodge-podge of humanity was one Mister Cimarron Gleason, a Creek Indian who had fully adopted the white man's ways. Unfortunately, since so many of his people had done the same, it was going to be difficult to ferret him out. Charlie didn't want to ask for his whereabouts, since that might alarm the outlaw. It was best for him to leave off his horse at a safe place, then scuffle around the town until he either located the man or picked up some information on him.

Obviously the highest segment of the society around him were the Creek people. Only they could own land according to federal law. The whites there were either drifters, desperados or ones who had found a way around the statutes by marrying Indian women, thus obtaining the right to property. The worst off were the blacks. They had been slaves and had yet to carve out a comfortable niche for themselves in this multi-racial populace. If there were a shovel or pick in sight, nine times out of ten there was a sweating black man at the end of it.

Charlie slowly wandered through the helter-kelter arrangement of the settlement. The fact that he had a shotgun in his hand only made him fit into the scene that much better. His bad limp did attract attention, but he hadn't seen Cimarron Gleason in so long, he doubted if the man would tie him into any talk about a gimp in town even if he heard one was around.

Most of the saloons were only planks laid across some barrels situated in front of a tent. Thus it was easy for Charlie to check the places out as he hobbled down what seemed to be a main street of sorts.

Several rough characters plainly looking for trouble sauntered through the throng. They each gave Charlie a quick glance and sized him up for possible amusement. A man in his physical condition could easily be bullied or pummeled into defeat but that would cause no admiration from the crowd—although some of the more sadistic thought it might be great sport. But the shotgun the limping man toted signified one thing: any confrontation with him would involve deadly force and none of the potential tormentors were in the mood for a situation that serious.

After an hour of hobbling around the area, Charlie's leg was so sore he could hardly move. He had sighted an outdoor café of sorts and he went back to it. The eatery was like the crude saloons except the counter was lower and there were wooden crates provided as seats. Charlie gratefully eased his weight down on one and signaled to the potbellied man who seemed to be running the place. "What's on yore menu?"

The cook wiped his nose. "Flapjacks an' coffee or coffee an' flapjacks. Take yore choice, pard."

Charlie didn't appreciate the humor. "I'll take a meal."

"Two bits . . . in advance."

"Two bits!" Charlie exclaimed at the outrageous price. He had never paid more than ten or fifteen cents for such a feed before.

"Flour an' coffee beans is dear in these parts," the man said without even the slightest hint of an apology. "You pay or go hongry. Suit yoreself."

Charlie paid and ordered his coffee in advance. It was served in a tin cup. He rubbed some specks of rust off the rim and sipped from it until the flapjacks were set in front of him. They were surprisingly light and delicious looking. He took a bite and found their taste equal to the appearance.

"Perty good, eh, stranger?" the cook asked. "If'n you try any other cafe here in Muskogee you won't find none better. Make up yore mind to git yore grub here as long as yo're hangin' around . . . an' got the money."

"I'll do that," Charlie said. He finished the meal and left the crude café to wander around some more.

As night fell the town's appearance changed. The crowd grew as did the activities. Hard-looking women tried to entice him into tents where canvas partitions separated the whores' bins. Meanwhile numerous gambling games were going full tilt as the clamor and shouting became a din. Now and then a senseless but brutal fist fight would erupt and either end quickly with a few heavy blows or with the appearance of knives. The sound of an occasional shot marked a possible death or wounding as the celebrating grew in intensity.

Charlie limped slowly as he methodically checked faces hoping for a glimpse of Cimarron. He was beginning to get bored when he was unexpectedly bumped into. A drunken cowboy snarled at him.

"Watch where yo're goin'!"

Charlie ignored him and started to step around the drover, but the drunk wouldn't let him. "I said fer you to watch it," the cowboy said. He grabbed Charlie's shoulder and threw a clumsy punch.

Charlie drove the butt of the shotgun into the man's belly, doubling him up. Then he drew his pistol and delivered a ringing clout to the side of his head. The reveler staggered off to the side into a crowd of gamblers around a faro table. The group angrily pummeled him, then pushed the reeling, bleeding drunk on down the row where he received similar treatment from another bunch gathered at a crude bar. This time he collapsed out of the way between two tents where he would be left in peace to recover as best he could.

Charlie gave up his search after midnight and went back to the corral where he mounted his horse. The wrangler on duty there, armed to the teeth, recognized him from his limp. "Have a good time tonight?"

"Not much," Charlie replied.

"It don't look like it," the wrangler said, noting that Charlie was stark staring sober.

"I reckon I'll git my bedroll and find a place over yonder to sleep," Charlie said indicating the dark area outside the settlement.

"You'll git yoreself killed out there," the wrangler warned him. "You can sleep right in here fer four bits—if'n you got a mind to."

Charlie instantly took the offer. The idea of being stabbed or bludgeoned by a robber combing the woods for victims didn't appeal to him. He forked over the money and found a place near the corral fence. He had some trouble drifting off to sleep as gunshots, shouts or the sudden high-pitched yell of an angry scarlet lady penetrated his restfulness.

But those weren't the only irritants keeping him from needed slumber. The image of Matilda Koch danced through his mind in an uneasily persistent way. She seemed slim and almost boyish in a way, but there was no denying a certain feminine charm that seemed appealing to him. He had been trying to stifle his thoughts about her all along, but now he realized that unbidden emotions were creeping into his life where the Caldwell landlady was concerned.

Finally fatigue and time wore at him until he sank into blissful sleep in the middle of wild, wicked Muskogee.

Early the next morning Charlie went directly back to the little eatery for breakfast. He had just gotten his order when the very man he was looking for appeared down the street.

Cimarron Gleason, leading his horse, ambled past him. The Indian had evidently just arrived in town after spending some time either traveling or camping. Charlie wasted no time. He got to his feet and stamped after the outlaw as quickly as he could.

"Hey!" the cook hollered from behind the counter. "Yo're gonna eat these cold if you don't hurry back."

Charlie wasn't worried about making noise as he approached Gleason. The crowd's activities made it impossible to hear a thing. He stomped up behind Gleason and raised the shotgun high. Then he brought it down with stunning force between the shoulder blades.

Gleason pitched forward and rolled over on his back with his eyes dazed and glassy. Charlie leaned his weight on his bad leg and kicked out quickly with the toe of the good one, catchin Gleason on the point of the chin. The outlaw's head snapped back and he collapsed in the mud. Without hesitating Charlie fetched his handcuffs from his pockets and, after turning the outlaw on his stomach, quickly snapped them on Gleason's wrists.

"Hey! You a lawman?" A surly buffalo hunter warily approached Charlie with his hand dangerously close to his pistol.

Charlie opened his vest to show he wore no star. "This is personal," he said. "The sonofabitch killed my pardner."

"Then why don't you jest shoot him?" the hunter asked.

Charlie leveled his shotgun dead on the man's chest. "You seem awful interested in what I'm doin'. You a pal o' his?"

The buffalo man's bravado disappeared when he noticed both Charlie's weapon and the fact that nobody in the crowd was going to back him up.

Gleason groaned and tried to sit up. His eyes still wore the blank look as consciousness edged through his clouded mind. Finally he was able to see relatively clearly and realized he had just been attacked. He looked up and for a few moments gaped at his assailant before speaking. "Charlie Martell! You sonofabitch!"

"In person," Charlie said grimly. "Git to yore feet, Cimarron."

"I cain't," the outlaw said. "Yo're gonna have to help me."

"I only got one good arm," Charlie said. "And it's busy. If you ain't up and movin' in five seconds I'll do the job here and now."

"Yo're gonna kill me on account o' Nolan, ain't

73

you?"

"As sure as hell's hot," Charlie said.

Cimarron struggled up and stood with his hands cuffed behind him. He looked aroun at the crowd imploringly. "This here feller was a lawman! He's gonna git me because I killed a starpackin' ol' pardner o' his."

"Move along," Charlie said, motioning with the shotgun. He hooked his bad arm through the reins of Gleason's horse.

Gleason obeyed but continued his appeal. "The feller I helped kill was tryin' to grab ol' Dandy Kilgallen."

"Shut up!" Charlie hissed. "An' don't worry none about Dandy. I laid him out in Caldwell a few weeks back."

Gleason turned in astonishment. "What're you talkin' about?"

"I called him out an' bested him," Charlie said with a tinge of pride in his voice.

"Harry Green wouldn't let you git away with that," Gleason said.

"Harry Green is tied up behind that damn star he's wearin'," Charlie said. "Now you keep movin'."

It didn't take them long to reach the corral where Charlie had left his own horse. Within minutes the wary wrangler, keeping a careful eye on Charlie's shotgun, produced the animal fully saddled and ready.

"How much I owe you?" Charlie asked.

"Er . . . nothin', mister."

"Hell, I ain't mad at you," Charlie said. "I'm mad at *him*! How much do I owe you?"

"Six bits oughta take care of it."

Charlie balanced the shotgun over his saddle and

kept a close eye on Gleason as he pulled the money from his pocket. Then he mounted and told the Creek to do the same. Without being asked, the other man helped him up into the saddle.

"Let's ride east," Charlie said.

"Why don't you go on ahead and shoot me here?" Gleason asked.

"I ain't fool enough to want witnesses even here in Muskogee," Charlie said.

"Since you called out Dandy and won, why not give me a chance at a fair fight?"

Charlie shook his head. "Them fellers that shot me up crippled me, they didn't make me stupid."

"Well, shit." Gleason sighed, accepting his fate. He knew his lifestyle offered little chance for a peaceful death in bed, but if the end was to be violent he preferred being shot to getting strung up on a gallows by a legal executioner or on a handy tree by an irate mob. Suddenly he laughed. "I reckon you know that word o' what jest happened will git around to some o' my friends. They'll come lookin' fer us."

"I been thinkin' on that," Charlie said.

Gleason settled down into sullen silence, knowing that if he continued to goad or nag at Charlie the end result would be another bashing from the shotgun. He waited until they had ridden for a couple of hours before he spoke again. "Why don't you go on and shoot me right now?" he asked. "Where the hell are we goin' anyway?"

"I really ain't gonna shoot you a'tall, Cimarron," Charlie said. "I'm takin' you to Fort Smith."

"To Judge Parker?"

"The same," Charlie said. "There's a warrant out fer you."

Gleason laughed. "By God, Charlie, I got to hand

it to you. There ain't a lawman this side o' hell that coulda got me outta Muskogee. Yo're prob'ly proud o' yoreself, ain't you?"

Charlie grinned at him without humor. "I don't figger I got much to be ashamed of."

Gleason smiled back just as viciously. "But like I said, Charlie, my friends is gonna hear about this. We got quite a ride afore we reach Fort Smith."

The moonlight was bright that night as it cast a yellow glow over the camp Charlie had set up along the Arkansas River. Their campfire had settled down into dull glowing embers and both bedrolls were stretched out and occupied. Cimarron Gleason was easily visible, his handcuffs attached to a chain that was wrapped around his saddle. Charlie Martell was rolled up tightly in his blankets, the covers thrown over his head. A gun barrel showed through the folds of the covers, giving evidence he was probably sleeping with one hand on the trigger ready for instant action if necessary.

The two men eased into the camp and halted immediately as Gleason's horse whinnied softly.

They waited until the animal settled down before they walked slowly up to the sleeping men. One pointed to Cimarron Gleason and his partner nodded as both then turned their pistols on Charlie's bedroll.

Then they fired.

The blankets jumped under the impact of the bullets. This was followed immediately by a shotgun exploding from the nearby bushes. One of the pistoleros took the full force of the blast that threw him completely over Gleason. The Creek Indian woke up violently and howled in rage and fright as the other gunman stood there stupidly looking around.

Charlie Martell stepped forward from the brush with his pistol drawn. He had it aimed dead on his attempted murderer, his crippled right hand steadying the barrel. He fired and missed.

The other man flicked off two quick wild shots that were hopeless. Charlie's next bullet bit flesh off the opponent's arm and spun him completely around to catch a gut shot that doubled him up and sat him down on the hot embers. He yelled and rolled off quickly, sitting back up just in time to catch a .45 slug in the forehead, which blew his brains out the back of his skull in a red-gray splash of tissue and blood. Then he collapsed backward, his legs drawing up in death.

"You got more'n two friends?" Charlie asked Gleason.

"Damn!" Gleason said, looking at the dead men.

"If not," Charlie went on without waiting for an answer, "the rest of our trip oughta be plumb uneventful."

Gleason looked at his dead friends in disbelief. "When did you git up and sneak off to them bushes?"

"Right after you dozed off," Charlie said. He picked through his bullet-riddled blankets. "They've ruined my sleepin' gear, though."

"Now ain't that jest too goddammed bad," Gleason said sarcastically.

"I reckon their horses ain't too far away," Charlie mused more to himself than Gleason. "Should be some stuff I can use to replace my own things." He started to walk off in the direction the men had come from, then he stopped and looked back at his prisoner. "I'll be back directly. You don't mind waitin', do you?"

"You go straight to hell, you no good sonofabitch!" Gleason yelled out. "If you was any kind o' man you'd shoot me too."

"That ain't the decent thing to do," Charlie said.

"What the hell's the difference?" Gleason asked. "They're gonna hang me in Fort Smith anyhow."

"It'll be legal," Charlie countered.

"I wanta tell you somethin,' Charlie," Gleason said. "I shot ol' Nolan Edgewater three, mebbe four times that day."

Charlie's jaw tightened and he instinctively drew his pistol as the hatred boiled up inside him. For several long seconds the barrel of the weapon was aimed dead on the Indian outlaw before it was lowered again.

"I don't want to hang," Gleason said. "It's been somethin' that's bothered me all along. Gittin' shot is what I always expected, but I cain't stand the thought o' bein' dropped at the end of a rope."

"Reconcile yourself to it," Charlie said. "I ain't shootin' no prisoner down."

"Goddam you, Charlie Martell, yo're still a starpacker at heart and always will be."

"Mebbe that's good and mebbe it's bad," Charlie said. "But at least I don't have to worry none 'bout gittin' hung, do I?"

"To answer yore question of a few minutes ago," Gleason said. "I *do* have more friends and whether you deliver me to Fort Smith or not got nothin' to do with them gittin' even with you. So you might not git hung, but yo're sure as hell gonna git shot!"

Charlie didn't answer as he walked into the night to look for the other outlaws' horses.

chapter 7

Fort Smith sat on the border between Arkansas and the Indian nations. It was the site of the federal court directed by Judge Isaac C. Parker, the magistrate who administered justice in the wild areas governed by the Indians.

Charlie Martell kept a wary eye on his desperate prisoner as they turned off the town's main street for the building that served as both courtroom and jail. The solid brick structure had once been the officers' quarters of the old fort, but was now the hub for Judge Parker and his marshals' operations. Charlie swung off his horse and beckoned at Gleason with his shotgun. The two suddenly noticed a strong disagreeable odor. Charlie sniffed the air. "Phew! Smells like the biggest shithouse in the world."

"It is," Gleason said sullenly. "But it's known as the U.S. jail in these parts." He indicated the steps that led down to the basement prison used to house prisoners waiting for trial.

"Yore home sweet home fer awhile," Charlie said as he pushed the Creek up the steps. The two crossed the porch and went inside to the marshal's office.

Heck Thomas sat at the desk laboriously writing out a report as the two entered. The husky, moustachioed lawman looked up at what obviously was a man and his prisoner. He slowly recognized the cripple holding the shotgun.

"Charlie Martell?"

"Howdy, Heck. It's been awhile."

"It sure as hell has," the lawman said as he stood up to offer his hand. "I see you ain't been jest a-layin' around."

"Nope. I got a prisoner to turn in. I heard there was a warrant out fer him."

"Yep. We been wantin' ol' Cimarron fer a spell now. But we couldn't figger a good way o' gittin him outta Muskogee without havin' to kill a dozen or so folks."

"I had to shoot a couple," Charlie said. "But I reckon he don't have as many good friends as he figgered."

Thomas looked at Charlie's bare shirt front. "You ain't packin' a badge?"

"Call it a citizen's arrest," Charlie said.

"Good enough," Thomas said. "I reckon this is on account o' Nolan Edgewater too, huh? By the way, yore reward money fer Dandy Kilgallen has been sent up there to Kansas."

"Good," Charlie said. "I already drawed on it from a local bank. They'll be glad to git it."

"I was surprised to hear you was back in action," Heck said. "Somebody tole me quite a while back that you was . . . well, sorta down on yore luck, Charlie."

"I was. But Nolan gittin' killed snapped me back together somehow."

"Let's lock up Cimarron here, then we can talk over some hot coffee," Thomas said. "I gotta let Judge Parker know he's been turned in, too. As a matter o' fact, I think the judge is gonna wanta palaver with you on all this, Charlie." ·

"Sure," Charlie said agreeably. "Fine with me."

Thomas's voice bellowed out for the jailer down in the basement as he began filling out the booking papers on the court's newest prisoner.

"If you two sons of bitches think I'm gonna jest sit around down in that hellhole and wait fer Parker to have me strung up, yo're both loco!" Gleason said.

Thomas's big hand shot out and slapped the Indian's face hard enough to stagger him back into Charlie's shotgun. The marshal scowled. "You speak with respect an' use the word 'sir' around here, you got that?"

"In that case," Gleason said. "You two sons of bitches are loco . . . *sir!*"

"That's better," Thomas said as he turned back to his paperwork. A burly marshal, obviously the jailer, walked in with a set of heavy handcuffs. Charlie wordlessly removed his own and they were quickly replaced by the others. Thomas finished off the booking form and waved toward the door. "Take him away, Ned." He stood up. "You ever met Judge Parker, Charlie?"

"Cain't say as I have," Charlie said.

"Well, I'm about to give you the privilege. C'mon." They went out into the hallway and crossed over to the courtroom where many a desperado had heard the grim sentence of death from the famous judge. Thomas led Charlie past the large, elevated desk to the door to the judge's chambers and knocked. "Yore Honor?"

"Yes, Heck. Please come in."

When he first caught sight of the judge Charlie was surprised. He had expected to see a fiery, evil-looking old cuss, but instead there sat a sensitive-

81

looking man with large, kindly eyes that belied the man's reputation as a merciless dispenser of justice. The judge nodded politely at Charlie, taking quick notice of his injuries as he limped up to his desk.

"Yore honor, I'd like to introduce a friend o' mine named Charlie Martell. He was the one that did in Dandy Kilgallen up in Kansas. An' he jest waltzed in here with Cimarron Gleason in custody on a citizen's arrest."

The judge smiled and stood up with an outstretched hand. "Well! I'm very pleased to meet you, Mister Martell. And may I thank you for the great service you have performed for us?"

"Yo're welcome," Charlie said.

"Charlie was a town marshal up in Wichita," Heck explained. "Got hisself shot up bad—as you can see, yore Honor—and I might as well explain away his grabbin' Cimarron and shootin' Dandy by jest sayin' that him an' Nolan Edgewater was mighty fine friends."

"I see," Parker said. "I believe the other man involved in Nolan's death was John Dougherty, true, Heck?"

"Yes, yore honor." He turned to Charlie. "You ain't got him yet by any chance, have you?"

"No," Charlie answered. "But I expect him to show up in Caldwell once he hears from Harry Green 'bout Dandy. I was figgerin' on waitin' fer him there."

"There is a warrant for Dougherty, naturally," Judge Parker said. "Would you care to serve it in the name of this court, Mister Martell?"

"I'd be glad to, yore honor," Charlie said. "But . . ." He held up his crippled hand.

"Your impairments seemed to do little to hinder

82

you in your besting of Messrs. Kilgallen and Gleason. However, I feel that even a healthy officer should take advantage of all the aid he can possibly muster. Would the local lawmen in Caldwell be of much help to you in apprehending John Dougherty?"

"None at all, yore honor," Charlie said. "The town marshal's been in a few brushes with the law hisself. Him and Dougherty are good friends anyhow."

The judge nodded knowingly. "I fear that many of my own marshals could not come out unscathed from a close investigation of their past lives, but it takes tough, determined men to administer the law in this part of the country."

"Yes, sir," Charlie said.

"I don't wish to be insensitive, Mister Martell, but can you shoot well?"

"Yes, sir. I had my shotgun altered to handle in my left arm, see?" He held it up. "An' I figgered out a way to shoot perty good left handed by holdin' my bad'un up to steady my pistol. I did a lot o' practicin'."

The judge was impressed. "Since you are obviously set on avenging Nolan's death, perhaps, as I mentioned before, you would care to do it under the authority of this court."

"Sir?"

"Charlie, his honor wants to swear you in as a U.S. deputy marshal and take a warrant with you on Dougherty," Heck interjected.

Charlie blinked hard. The idea of actually wearing a badge again and riding back to Kansas as a working law officer staggered him for a moment or two.

"He'll do it," Heck answered for him. "An' he's the logical man, too. Like he said, Dougherty's gonna be goin' to Caldwell to look fer him. All he has to do is sit there and wait."

"I would like him brought back here alive for trial," Judge Parker said. Far from being the insensitive executioner that many thought him to be, Isaac Charles Parker was a well-educated man with a deep intellect coupled to a great understanding of the law and its intent. His sole purpose in accepting he post at Fort Smith was to be the driving force in establishing decency and order so that the area might begin to prosper as good people, convinced they could safely go about their business, would move in and add their valued presence to the territory.

Charlie shrugged. "I'll try, yore honor, but I know Dougherty from Wichita. He's mean as hell and his good friend Harry Green is marshal of Caldwell. I cain't see a reason fer him to surrender to me, unless he's shot up bad."

"We live in brutal times, Mister Martell, and must deal with men who are little better than beasts. I commend you on your lawful treatment of Cimarron Gleason by bringing him to justice in a proper manner despite your personal hatred for the man. All I can ask is that you attempt to apprehend Dougherty in a peaceful manner. I'm sure you know what to do if he resists."

"And he will, yore honor," Heck said.

Parker nodded. "You're undoubtedly correct, Heck. Have my clerk come in and we'll get about the business of swearing in and preparing Mister Martell for his mission."

"Ready to go to work, Charlie?" Heck asked.

"I sure am—except fer my horse. The one I got is from a livery in Wichita. I got to take him back."

"We have mounts confiscated from outlaws," the judge said. "I'll authorize one to be assigned to you, Marshal Martell."

Marshal Martell!

Charlie hoped the judge and Heck didn't notice how his eyes nearly watered with emotion as his chest swelled with new pride and confidence.

Charlie eased the horse down into a cottonwood grove along the river bank. His leg was throbbing badly as a way of complaining about the days of mistreatment and neglect. The twisted muscles that needed the relaxing stimulus of heat had drawn up tight and now were badly cramped.

He swung out of the saddle and hitched up the horses, then sat down by the water and rubbed the stiff limb gently. He felt a little relief as the circulation of blood increased in the sore areas. Closing his eyes, he let his mind drift away from the hurt. He was so far out of himself within a few minutes that he was completely, and blissfully, unaware of his physical surroundings.

"Hold it there, you sonofabitch!"

Charlie's hands flew up automatically and he heard several pairs of boots coming down the bank toward him. He started to turn.

"Keep yore eyes to the front!"

Charlie did as he was told as he waited. Within seconds three gunhawks stood in front of him, two with pistols and a third with a carbine leveled dead on his chest.

"Is that him, Hal?"

"Sure is," a blond pistolero said. "Took ol' Cimarron right outta Muskogee with him. An' prob'ly shot Ellsworth and Young, too."

85

The third individual, the carbine man, nudged Charlie with the business end of his piece. "Did you turn our pal over to Parker?"

Charlie decided not to answer and this earned him a quick poke in the jaw that sent him rolling down to the river. Infuriated, he struggled to his feet as quickly as possible, the effort causing hot stabs of pain through his leg. He cursed, but wisely kept his hands up as the three looked down on him.

"We asked if you turned Cimarron in an' shot our pals . . . an' don't lie to us. We damn near caught up to you two afore you crossed into Arkansas. So we been waitin' fer you to ride back into the Injun country."

"I . . ."

"Hey! He's wearin' a badge!" the blond man interrupted. He walked forward and grabbed the piece of metal pinned to Charlie's shirt. "A U.S. deputy . . . outta Hangin' Judge Parker's court, ain't you?"

"I am," Charlie said.

"So yo're a lawman after all. They said in Muskogee you wasn't."

"I didn't have a badge then," Charlie said. "But I got one now."

"An' we're gonna shoot you right through it," the carbine man said. "Then pin it on yore ass," he added with a laugh.

"That's our style o' doin' in starpackers," the third man said.

"Hold it, boys, shootin' this bastard is too good fer him," the blond said. "Let's string him up jest like ol' Hangin' Parker is gonna do to Cimarron."

"Good idee," the carbine man said. He motioned to Charlie. "Git yore gimpy ass up to them taller trees. *Move!*"

Charlie negotiated the slippery bank with some difficulty while his potential murderers followed. As he limped past the horse from the Wichita livery he suddenly reached out and pulled the reins that bound the animal to the tree. Then he yelled and spun on his heel and smacked the brute's flank hard with the flat of his hand. The old horse leaped forward and ran into the three outlaws who were trapped in the confined space that led up from the river. The impact sent them sprawling as Charlie took a half dozen shuffling steps to the government horse. He pulled the shotgun from its boot and quickly retraced his uneven steps. The carbine man got to his feet first and looked up just in time to see Charlie leveling down on him with those two big barrels.

"Oh, damn!"

The outlaw took the blast in the upper chest and flew down to the river like he'd been propelled by steam. His body splashed into the water and thrashed around for several seconds in the reddening foam before it stiffened, then relaxed in death.

The blond fired at Charlie from an awkward sitting position. The newly sworn-in marshal had already drawn his pistol. He hit the pistolero once in the shoulder and twice in the chest as another shot socked into a nearby tree.

One to go, but where was he?

Charlie quickly edged into the poor concealment of the heavy brush and stood still, barely breathing as he listened carefully. All he could hear was the running river and the hooves of the old horse as he clomped back to stand by the other animal. He looked past his mounts and could see where the outlaws had tied up theirs some distance away. The third man had a couple of choices, it seemed. He could attempt an escape by a dash from the grove of trees or he could stay and fight. Charlie tried to figure which alternative he would choose.

The question was answered by a shot that chipped bark off the tree just above his head, and just as quickly the second bullet passed so close Charlie could feel it zip past his nose. He dropped to the ground and crawled awkwardly but rapidly deep into the trees, dragging his bad leg behind him.

Charlie reholstered the pistol and broke open the shotgun to remove the spent shells. After quickly reloading, he began to put an old saying into practice: *The best defense is a good offense.*

He was on his feet now, every fiber of his being bristling with anticipation and alertness. He was glad he hadn't eaten that day. Charlie always figured he was keener and sharper with an empty belly. Sort of went back to man's primitive days, he thought, when hunger made him a better hunter.

A tree limb exploded into bits over his head and Charlie turned toward the sound and blew off both barrels. Vegetation flew as the pellets streaked through the brush.

Then silence.

A sudden cracking of a limb to the right, and again Charlie's shotgun roared through the afternoon air. Dust and bits of leaves floated in the trees, but no yells of pain or anger.

More silence.

The stock of the shotgun literally splintered into pieces simultaneously with the explosion of the shot. Charlie was barely able to maintain his grip on the weapon. He caught sight of his quarry's shirt through the tangled limbs a few feet away. He fired awkwardly with the ruined weapon and it flew out of his hands to somersault itself several feet behind him. He started to draw his pistol as the gunman leaned out from behind a tree. The man's face was white as chalk, unnatural-looking. Charlie's pistol was in his hand so fast he hadn't realized he had drawn it and he was firing in that manner of his with the crippled hand steadying the barrel. His final three bullets found their marks but the man didn't fall. He merely swung back and forth under the impact of the slugs. Curious, Charlie edged forward, but the outlaw made no overt move. As he drew closer, Charlie could see the man was obviously dead.

He walked around the tree that concealed the gunman and nearly vomited.

His shotgun blast had blown the third assailant completely in half. Somehow the torso had caught in the low fork of one of the trees while the legs had been blown some dozen feet away. One foot was still twitching in an obscene gesture of death. Charlie left the hunks of meat where they were and went back to resume his trip north.

Now he had three more horses (that now legally and properly belonged to the U.S. government), as well as the belongings of the three outlaws. He took time to go through their things and was surprised at their apparent poverty. The horses were lean and mistreated, while aside from some filthy bedrolls there wasn't much worth taking. Their weapons were the only things of value and Charlie gathered them up into one of the saddlebags before he mercifully unsaddled and freed the outlaws' miserable horses. Then he remounted and turned once again for Kansas.

He rode deep in thought, suddenly realizing that the years he had spent as a drunk and feeling sorry for himself were worse than empty ones—they were *wasted*. All that time he had the potential to overcome his injuries and return to his job as a lawman. It would have taken hard work, as he now knew, and some convincing of other folks (not all people, unfortunately, were as open-minded or had as keen a perception of their fellow man as Judge Parker). Every drunken binge and humiliation he had experienced had been a useless burden to bear. U.S. Deputy Marshal Charles Houston Martell suddenly realized that he had overcome his infirmities and that in doing so he had become a better man now than he had ever been.

But he wasn't dumb enough to think he had become immortal. He still had John Dougherty and Harry Green to face, and the quicker man, crippled or not, would be the survivor.

chapter 8

Orv Pickett walked out of the livery barn's large doors and grinned widely as Charlie rode up. "By God!" he exclaimed. "We sure been hearin' things about you here in Wichita."

"Howdy," Charlie said. He dismounted and handed the reins of the old gray to Orv. "I'm returnin' the horse you loaned me."

"Hell, Charlie, I'm proud yo're usin' him."

"I got this other'n when I was swore in as marshal at Fort Smith," Charlie said. "Thank you jest the same."

"Yeah! We heard about that. It was in the *Eagle* an' ever'thing. A nice write-up about you, Charlie. Come by telegraph from Arkansas about you arrestin' Cimarron Gleason and turnin' him in. 'Course we heard about you gunnin' down Dandy Kilgallen afore that." Orv shook his head in wonder. "Boy, yo're really the ol' Charlie we used to know, ain't you? Got on some damn nice store-bought clothes and yore skinny face is filled out some—got good healthy color, too. Looks like yo're just about right back where you started."

Charlie smiled a little despite himself. "I suppose so . . . just a mite slower, that's all."

"Maybe walkin', but not gunnin'!" Orv said.

91

"How 'bout boardin' my horse fer a day or two?" Charlie asked. "I got some business here in Wichita."

"Hell, yes, Charlie!"

Charlie pulled his saddlebags free and settled them across his shoulders before he waved a goodbye and clumped back to the street.

His first stop was the gunsmith. He wordlessly pushed the shotgun with its shattered stock across the counter. "Can you fix it?"

The craftsman, a German, smiled and nodded. "Sure t'ing, Marshal. Ve heard you vas back in action again."

"Yeah," Charlie answered. "One thing I want to go over with you." He laid out the leather padding he had gotten in Caldwell. "I want that stock three inches shorter'n usual and this mounted on it."

The gunsmith nodded with sudden understanding. "Shoot her vit' one hand, eh, Marshal?"

"You got it."

"T'is vill take a couple, maybe t'ree days."

A sudden regret at this delay in getting back to Matty Koch welled up in him. But Charlie tried to ignore it. "Fine," he said agreeably. "I'll check in with you day after tomorrow." He couldn't afford to wait to get back to Caldwell before having it fixed. Dougherty might already be there planning his ambush with Harry Green.

When Charlie left the shop he noted that people on the street eyed him closely as he scuffled down the boardwalks. This was like the good old days as far as he was concerned. He would take no guff from any man now and no wise one would offer any. He turned into the town marshal's office. "I got business here," he announced to the deputy at the desk.

The law officer, the same youngster who had been there the last time he was at the jail, looked up in happy surprise. "Howdy, Mister Martell."

"*Marshal* Martell," Charlie corrected him curtly and pointed to his badge.

"Oh, yes, sir, Marshal. What can I do fer you?"

"First thing I want to do is file a report involvin' three jaspers that tried to drygulch me in the Injun country."

"Sure thing, mister, er . . . Marshal. Let me git a pencil and you give me the particulars. Then I'll write it up real nice in ink."

"Fine," Charlie said, settling down uninvited in a nearby chair. "Then I want a report of the incident telegraphed down to the U.S. court at Fort Smith, Arkansas."

The young lawman sat poised over a sheaf of papers. "Start talkin'—slow, if you please—and I'll git her all down here good and proper."

Charlie spoke in a deliberate monotone. "While on my way to Kansas to serve a warrant duly give me by his honor Judge Isaac C. Parker I was jumped by three hardcases I ain't never seen before. They claimed they was pals o' Cimarron Gleason who I had arrested and turned in to the U.S. court at Fort Smith, Arkansas. One of 'em was a big ol' husky blond feller about twenty-seven or twenty-eight years old. The second was a short, skinny jasper in his forties with grayin' hair. The final 'un was heavyset, 'bout the same age as the second, with thinnin' sandy hair. I killed all three and left 'em there. Their horses was blowed and wore so I turned 'em aloose. There was no personal gear, other'n a couple o' guns, worth the U.S. government to worry 'bout. Respectfully submitted, C.H. Martell, United

93

States Deputy Marshal."

"I got it all, Marshall, ever' word," the kid said.

"Fine. Have y'all hard anything involvin' a John Dougherty hereabouts or maybe over in Caldwell?"

"Cain't say that we have, Marshal," the young lawman replied. "I know the name, though. That Dougherty likes to shoot first, then discuss the situation second. 'Cept the other feller generally ain't in any shape fer conversation."

Charlie nodded. "Yeah. Well, I'll be around Wichita two or three days and I'll check in now and then."

"Sure thing, Marshal. You gonna be over at the livery stable?"

Charlie shot him a mean glance that caused the younger man to nearly cringe. "I'll have a *hotel room.*"

"Yes, sir!"

Charlie went outside and stood for several moments surveying the street. He nodded politely to people who greeted him as they walked by. Then he slowly hobbled down to Sly Webster's Tonsorium.

"Howdy, Charlie!" Sly said happily as Charlie entered his establishment. The man who was getting his hair cut lifted a hand in greeting under the sheet that covered him.

"I thought I'd use yore bath," Charlie said.

"I'll git her ready directly," Sly said.

"That's all right," Charlie said, sitting down in one of the chairs. "I can wait."

"I don't mind, Marshal," the customer said. "There's nothin' fer me to rush about."

"I said I'd wait," Charlie said with a finality that convinced the two that further conversation was useless.

Sly happily snipped away as he talked. "By God,

Charlie, we been hearin' excitin' things about you. I reckon you just about cleaned out the saloon down at Caldwell."

"Somebody's exaggeratin'," Charlie said. "I shot Dandy Kilgallen. Nobody else drawed on me."

"I cain't git over it. But by God, we're proud as hell o' you," Sly said sincerely. "I tell folks around here how you an' me was always friends."

"Yeah, that's true," Charlie said. "You showed me some consideration when other people didn't."

Sly stopped and looked serious. "You know, Charlie, when I mention how you took supper with us lots o' times, there's some here in Wichita think I'm a damn liar."

"Well, they're wrong," Charlie said. "I reckon I ate over at yore house on many an occasion."

"You see?" Sly said pointedly to the man in the chair.

"Hell, I never said you was a liar!" the man protested.

"Anyhow, ol' Charlie here's a lawman again and I reckon jest as fast with a gun as always," Sly said. He pulled the sheet from his client and brushed the hairs off the man's shoulders. "That'll be fifteen cents."

The man paid, then started to settle down in a chair to talk for awhile, but Sly opened the door for him. "I'm gonna have to tend to the marshal now. I know he don't want to wait."

The customer took the hint, but paused in the door long enough to say goodbye to Charlie before he left. The lawman stood up. "I can sure use a hot soak."

"C'mon in the back," Sly said. As they started for the rear of the establishment the door opened and the barber's wife entered.

95

"Sly, I'm gonna need . . ." She stopped at the sight of Charlie and smiled. "Why, Mister Martell, how nice to see you! An' don't you look grand in them new clothes!"

"Thank you kindly," Charlie said. "Nice to see you again, Mrs. Webster."

Alma Webster was fairly bubbling. "You must come to supper tonight, Mister Martell. How does fried chicken sound to you?"

"Well . . ."

"By God!" Sly said happily. "Jest wait'll folks hear that U.S. Marshal Charlie Martell is eatin' at our place tonight."

"Mrs. Webster . . ."

"Oh, we've knowed each other for years! Call me Alma, please."

"Come on by the shop at closin' time," Sly said. "We'll walk on over to the house jest like we used to."

Charlie sighed. "Why, yes, I'll be happy to. I'm obliged, Mrs. . . . er, Alma."

"That's better, Charlie," she said. She turned to her husband. "Sly, I'll need a dollar fer shoppin'. You run off this mornin' without leavin' me a cent."

"Sure, darlin'," the barber said, fishing around in his pockets for the money. "Now you git three o' the fattest hens you can find. Me and Charlie's really gonna have appetites, ain't we, Charlie?"

"Yes, I reckon," Charlie said.

"That's exactly what I'm lookin' forward to," Alma said. She went to the door and paused before leaving. "You do look mighty nice dressed like that, Charlie."

"Thank you kindly," Charlie said.

"Now let's git to that bath," Sly said, taking his

arm. "I'll have you fit and spry within a half hour, Charlie, you wait an' see."

Charlie's stay in Wichita dissolved into three days of hot soaks, suppers with the Websters and constant checking in with both the gunsmith and the marshal's office before he was ready to leave for Caldwell.

That final morning, just at daylight, he saddled the horse, then impetuously stomped over to his old bunk. It was still there, although now only a wooden frame, but it looked even worse than he remembered it. He leaned back on his bad leg and kicked out with the good one, splintering the contraption into pieces that flew up against the wall.

There would be no more of that sort of thing.

Charlie hitched the horse to the rail in front of the marshal's office and went inside. Harry Green was dozing with his feet propped up on the desk. Charlie reached out and roughly shook one boot. The marshal snorted and opened his eyes.

Charlie looked down on him. "I'm here on official business."

Green rubbed his eyes, then grinned when he recognized Charlie. "Yeah. I heard tell you been made a U.S. marshal. Congratulations. Anything in particular I can do fer you?"

"I got a warrant fer John Dougherty," Charlie said. "Since he's a old pard o' yores I figgered you might know where he is."

"Damn, Charlie, I don't know where he *is,* but I sure as hell know where he's gonna *be,*" Green said. "An' that's right here, smack in the middle o' Caldwell, Kansas."

"You sure o' that?" Charlie asked.

"As sure as I know there's shit in a donkey," Green said. "Seems ol' John's really riled at you fer shootin' Dandy down. He was rather fond o' that feller. An' I know damn well he's heard by now 'bout you turnin' Cimarron Gleason in to that hangin' judge in Arkansas. I reckon that John Dougherty figgers he's got the best reasons in the world to gun you down."

"He's picked a good place fer it, if he comes to Caldwell," Charlie said in a calm voice. "Especially since the town marshal happens to be his pal and is the biggest backshootin' sonofabitch in the state o' Kansas."

Green's face whitened with anger. His eyes narrowed as he stood up. "You listen to me, Charlie Martell. U.S. marshal or no, yo're gonna end yore days on the streets o' Caldwell. An' when Dougherty comes to shoot, he never comes without no backup."

"Will that be you?" Charlie asked pointedly.

"Not this time."

"In that case I'll deal with you when I'm finished with Dougherty and his bunch. I still owe you fer Nolan Edgewater."

"I never took part in that shootin'," Green said.

"You didn't try to stop it neither," Charlie said. "And as far as I'm concerned yo're just as guilty as the others."

"Like I said before, Charlie, I owe you, so I'll be lookin' forward to it. But when Dougherty an' his pals git done with you, there ain't gonna be a piece left big enough to put a .45 slug into."

"You talk a hell of a gunfight," Charlie said. "Looks like there's gonna be a lot o' braggin' comin' to the test soon."

"I don't think you'll pass," Green said to Charlie's

back as he limped from the office.

Matty Koch and her maid were boiling sheets in the backyard when Charlie rode up. Matty's auburn hair was mussed and damp from the steam and wisps of it blew in the gentle breeze that wafted across the area from the prairie. She smiled in delight. "Why, Mister Martell! Now nice to see you again."

"Howdy, Mrs. Koch," he said. He felt a surge of happiness at the sight of the willowy woman and he found her smile absolutely wonderful. "The mornin' I left, you said somethin' about keepin' a room fer me."

"I surely did." Matty said. "An' it's waitin' right where it's always been."

"I was wonderin' if I could keep my horse here with yores instead of at the livery." He patted his marshal's badge. "I'm here on official business and might have to ride out in a hurry."

"Surely," she said. She pointed to the small corral with an open-sided shed that served as a stable of sorts. "It ain't much, but I reckon a horse won't mind, will he?"

"Not this one," Charlie said as he dismounted. "He was rode by a outlaw in the Injun country before the law got him. The government is lettin' me use him since I was appointed as a U.S. marshal."

"We seen that in the *Wichita Eagle*," Matty said. "One o' them railroad men brought it back from there. Seems you been makin' quite a name fer yoreself. Or should I say remakin' it?"

"I reckon," Charlie said. "But folks have a tendency to exaggerate."

"You put yore horse away and go on up and settle in," Matty said. "There's a pot o' coffee on the stove if you've a mind fer it."

"That sounds mighty good," Charlie said. He led the horse into the rickety corral and relieved the animal of its burden of saddle and other gear. As he walked back toward the house he paused and watched the women at work. "Y'all want some help?" he offered.

"No, thank you, Mister Martell," Matty said.

"Them wet sheets look a mite heavy," he said.

"We'll manage. You go on in the house. We'll be havin' supper in a coupla hours."

"Yes, Ma'am." Charlie did as she bid him and lugged his gear up to the second floor room where he had stayed before. The place had obviously been scrubbed down more than once during his absence, and the bed coverings and curtains were sparkling clean. Charlie sat his belongings down in the corner and settled on the bed. Its softness was inviting after the trip down from Wichita. He leaned back and closed his eyes, then the picture of Matty Koch appeared in his mind.

Even with her hair sort of messed up the way it was, she didn't seem too bad-looking.

chapter 9

A lantern flickered faintly in the kitchen as Charlie sat at the table sipping coffee. His thoughts were occupied with the coming gunfight with John Dougherty and any other individuals that might number between two and five—at least by Charlie's estimates. There was no doubt that Dougherty would first contact Green to get any information he might need to track down Charlie. A standup gunfight was out of the question. Neither of the antagonists was stupid enough to make a duel-like appointment for the confrontation.

For the first time since he'd gotten into this situation, Charlie began having a conscious, undeniable desire to remain alive. The suicidal drive that had impelled him to take up this quest for vengeance had died out, but not the original intent of the mission.

And there was this constant thinking of Matty Koch to contend with.

It was bad enough for a man to have some deadly confrontation on his mind without his mental processes being blocked by the images of a certain woman. Charlie couldn't call her pretty by any stretch of the imagination, but she was a hell of a ways off from being homely, too. She was a freckled, skinny woman in her thirties. Her hands were rough and red from the demands of maintaining a boarding house and she sure didn't move around with much feminine grace. For the life of him, Charlie couldn't figure out what he found so attractive about Matty, but more and more he had to admit that an infatuation was building up in him.

"Mister Martell?"

He looked up startled and saw Matty standing in the kitchen doorway. He smiled, not in his usual way, but with genuine pleasure. "Evenin', Ma'am."

She walked into the kitchen with that boyish gait of hers. "I was jest wonderin' who was in here."

"I spotted this here pot o' coffee and figgered I'd finish her off," Charlie said.

"I'd be pleased to brew up some more if you'd care fer fresh," she offered.

"Don't trouble yoreself," Charlie said. "This is jest fine."

"Mind if I join you?"

"I'd be pleased, Ma'am."

She sat down beside him. "I couldn't sleep tonight. I been a mite restless lately."

"Me too," Charlie said.

"I don't imagine! I hear you got some trouble comin' yore way," Matty said. "Ain't you scared?"

"Sure am."

"I'd think if a feller'd been shot before, he'd avoid it like the plague," she said. "It'd be smarter if you . . . well, cleared out 'til this thing blowed over. Then you could come on back and . . . well, live here in Caldwell. Maybe git a job or somethin'."

"Sounds mighty temptin'," he said. "But I got to see this Dougherty thing right to the final shot. Though I got to admit I don't much like the idea of bein' on the receivin' end of it."

She looked pointedly at his maimed hand. "You sure've had yore share."

He held up the useless member. "Awful lookin', ain't it?"

She surprised him by reaching out and taking it. "It's awful cold."

"I ain't surprised. It don't move much—matter o' fact it don't move a'tall."

"Can you feel anything with it?" she asked.

"Nope. She's numb as can be. I could stick pins in it, if I wanted to. I reckon it looks that way 'cause it's dead."

"It ain't dead," she said. "There's blood goin' through it or it'd rot. My grandpa had two fingers like this. He hauled off and hit some feller and busted his hand up somethin' terrible. Dang near killed the other man. That jasper walked around kinda silly fer the rest of his life."

"Yore grandpa musta been a powerful puncher."

"I think he was just good and mad," Matty said. "But he used to move them fingers with his other hand all the time. Massage 'em like. He said it kept the blood racin' through 'em and the skin was always healthy lookin'."

"Maybe that's what I oughta do . . ." He stopped speaking as Matty began pulling gently at the fingers. It took some effort but she got them open, then she rubbed easily as she slowly increased the pressure.

"Why looky there!" Charlie marveled. "There is some color gettin' in there."

"Sure is," Matty agreed. "You can see that even in the lantern light. But them fingers is sure hard to keep open."

"Maybe hot water'd loosen 'em up," Charlie suggested. "That always works with my leg."

"I'll heat some up," Matty said. Before he could protest she had gone to the sink and dipped some water from the bucket and poured it into a pan. Then she set it on the stove and poked at the coals to bring them to life.

"I don't want you to go to no trouble," Charlie said.

"It ain't no trouble to heat up a bit o' water," Matty said. "I just got to watch it so it don't git too hot."

"What's the differ'nce?" Charlie asked. "I couldn't feel it no how."

"Well, we still don't want to cook it, do we?"

"I reckon not."

For the next hour, Matty worked at the hand with soaks between patient massaging. She finally was able to hold the fingers open without difficulty as the tendons relaxed and stretched under the treatment.

"I can even see the veins now," Charlie said.

"Yep," she agreed. "The blood is gushin' through there. If we do this ever' night it won't be long 'til it looks like a healthy hand."

"It'll still be drawed up, though," Charlie said.

"But the color'll be good."

"Yeah. I reckon yo're right," he said. "Say, maybe I'd better check on the horses."

"I think I'll go with you," Matty said. "Maybe a little fresh air'll bring on sleep."

They went out back to the small corral and stood by the fence. The prairie moon was a bright yellow, its brilliance so strong it cast shadows. They said nothing as the peacefulness of the scene dictated silence. Charlie looked over at Matty. In the moonlight her face was softened and more feminine. He took note of her eyes with the aristocratic arch of the brows that gave her countenance a look of beauty in the soft light. She smiled at him as he edged closer.

Charlie slipped his arms around her and she grasped him around the waist, pulling her head into his shoulder. He reached down and tilted her face up, then kissed her tenderly. Her mouth, that seemed so thin and grim at times, was soft and full to him as she responded to his affections. They reluctantly broke off the contact.

"I been wantin' to do that fer a spell," Charlie said.

"And I been wantin' you to," Matty said.

"I got to tell you, Matty, I'm serious. I ain't doin' this fer amusement."

"I pray so, Charlie," she said, once again closing in to him. "Leastways it's pleasant when these feelin's is mutual."

"I ain't got much to offer a woman," Charlie said. "I'm busted up some, but I'm gettin' over it. The only thing is my line o' work."

"There's always the boardin' house," Matty said. "The haulin' and totin' around here is enough to keep any man busy."

"At any rate I cain't do nothin' 'til Dougherty is took care of."

"Oh, Charlie, you forgit him!" she exclaimed. "His kind always come to a bad end anyhow."

"I cain't, as much as I'd like to," Charlie said. "I been swore in as a U.S. marshal and charged with bringin' him in."

"Then quit! There ain't no law says you got to wear a badge," Matty countered.

"Judge Parker is a fine gentleman, Matty," Charlie said. "He showed confidence in me where many another feller had doubts. I cain't be so disrespectful to a good man like that."

Matty relented. She knew this kind of masculine pride and honor. The males in her own family lived stubbornly with a code of conduct so puzzling and irrational that even they couldn't explain it. They only honored the principles.

And sometimes they died for them.

The morning was still cool and pleasant as Charlie stepped out on the porch of the boarding house. His left hand held the shotgun as he warily let his eyes drift along the street, searching out areas between the dwellings and other potential concealment in bushes and even trees. Satisfied that all was normal, he shuffled down the steps and out the gate, turning toward the business section of town.

The residential area where Matty's place was located had a pleasant aura about it. The street was wide and the houses sat well apart. Even if it were part of a town, an outdoorsman like Charlie Martell felt he could breathe some. The buildings, all frame, were well cared for with shrubs and flower gardens as well as the inevitable picket fences marking property lines that separated neighbors. The ravages of the previous winter had been painted over—or just touched up, if that was all required—until even the outhouses looked spanking new and bright. The citizens of Kansas were an industrious bunch.

Charlie heard a horse coming down the street from his rear, so he stopped and backed up against a fence to watch the rider pass. As he approached, Charlie could see it was an Indian boy in his late teens. The swarthy face was dignified and unemotional despite the youth of its owner. His hair was cut short under the Montana peak he wore, and his white-man's clothing seemed well cared for. So did the pistol in his holster.

Charlie stared dead at him, letting the youth know he had acquired his full unwavering attention. The boy looked back just as unabashed as he drew up alongside. He nodded politely. "Howdy."

"Howdy," Charlie replied as the Indian rode by. Then he once again started on his way.

The first shot split one of the slats in the fence behind Charlie and the second went straight up into the air as the boy's horse whirled in fright at the sudden noise.

Charlie brought the shotgun up and cut loose. The shot struck the kid's leg but most of it went into the animal, which shrieked long and loud as it collapsed to the dirt, carrying its rider down and pinning him under the shuddering carcass.

Charlie approached the boy warily, pistol drawn and ready, but the kid was already in shock. The leg was blown nearly away just below the knee, yet Charlie scarcely paid his assailant's injury any mind as he pulled the pistol from the Indian's limp hand. Several people came running from their houses and Charlie could hear Matty's voice loud and coming fast toward him.

"Charlie! *Charlie!*"

He turned to comfort her and was somewhat surprised to see that she was carrying a Winchester .44 carbine—and the way she toted the weapon showed she was quite familiar with it. He held up his hand in a calming gesture. "Ever'thing's fine, Matty."

"Is that the man yo're lookin' for?" she asked. Then she inspected the wounded boy. "He's a Injun . . . and just a kid."

107

"I don't know who he is," Charlie said. He turned to one of the men standing there in his shirt sleeves. "Go on and git the doctor quick."

Within moments people from the business district came down for a look. By the time Charlie had applied a tourniquet to the boy's leg, Marshal Harry Green pushed his way through the growing crowd. "How'd it happen, Charlie?"

"Danged if I can figger it out," Charlie said. "The kid rode past me, then the next thing I knowed he was shootin'. I never seen him before."

"Looks familiar, but I cain't place him," Green said. "But it appears you damn near took his leg off."

"Killed the horse, huh?" Charlie asked.

"Yeah. You wouldn't think it could happen, but I reckon you struck his vitals and he went fast." Suddenly Green became the efficient lawman. "I don't think we can wait fer the doctor. Couple o' you fellers pick the boy up and take him on in. He's lookin' more 'n more peaked by the minute."

Charlie took Matty's arm. "I'll walk you on home." Then, over his shoulder to Green, "See you in a few minutes."

"Sure, Charlie."

"You say you didn't even know that boy?" Matty asked.

"First time I laid eyes on him," Charlie answered. He indicated the Winchester with a nod of his head. "You know how to use that thing?"

"I hope to spit in yore cuspidor I do!"

Charlie laughed. "Maybe I'll have to use you for my backup when Dougherty shows up."

"Don't make fun o' me," Matty chided him. "There's one feller in the grave and a couple walkin' around with lead in 'em that trifled with womenfolk

108

in my family."

"I believe that," Charlie said, stopping at the gate. "I'm goin' on uptown and see what this was all about . . . if the kid don't die first."

"You just be careful, Charlie Martell," Matty said angrily, as if he had planned the whole affair just to upset her.

"Yes, Ma'am."

When Charlie arrived at the doctor's office there was the usual crowd of curiosity seekers and just plain loafers gathered outside. They respectfully parted for him as he went in. Harry Green was in the waiting parlor, looking through the door to the doctor's treatment room.

"How's he doin'?" Charlie asked.

"The doc says he's got to take that leg off. There wasn't enough left to patch together. You gonna charge the Injun with anything if he lives?"

Charlie shook his head. "Nope. He's lost a leg so I'll call it square. What about local charges from yore office?"

"I reckon not," Green said. "But I don't want ever' damn range bum around to git the idea he can come into Caldwell and start a ruckus."

Charlie laughed without humor. "Almost sounds like yo're tryin' to run a clean town, Harry."

"I *am* runnin' a clean town," Green shot back. "Just 'cause I don't let some pushy goddammed U.S. marshal roust my personal friends around don't mean I ain't in control here."

"You ain't gonna charge me with anything, are you?"

Green answered with a disgusted look, then turned his attention back to the treatment area. "How's he doin', Doc?"

Doctor Orville Hubble was an overworked physician who served the area as best he could. Most of his patients were in a bad way by the time they decided to come in and see him. Broken bones, gunshot wounds, knife cuts and venereal diseases made up the bulk of his practice. "These Indians are a hardy bunch," he responded as he worked. "I could swear he is recovering at this moment, and the leg isn't completely amputated as of yet."

"I'm gonna want to talk with him," Charlie said.

"Come back this evening," the doctor advised him. "I think he'll be sufficiently coherent and sensible by then."

"Thanks," Charlie said. "I'll be here around eight." He left abruptly and scuffled through the crowd, ignoring the questions they asked him.

"My name is Amos Gleason," the boy said, looking wan and tired from the bed.

"How come you shot at me?" Charlie asked directly.

"Revenge."

"Revenge, hell! I don't even know you, boy."

"It's on account o' you they're gonna hang my cousin."

"What cousin?"

"Cimarron Gleason," Amos said. "Judge Parker sentenced him not a week ago."

Marshal Harry Green, who had been sitting on a chair next to the wall, got up and came over to the bed. "By God, no wonder you look familiar to me. You favor ol' Cimarron quite a bit."

"I know you," Amos said. "But you prob'ly don't remember me. I was just a tad when you was down at my pa's farm once a long time back."

"There was lots o' kids there," Green said.

"Well, Cimarron was my favorite cousin and now they're gonna hang him . . . thanks to *you*," Amos said, glaring at Charlie.

Chrlie shrugged. "The owlhoot trail's got a bitter end for most, kid. It cost Cimarron his life and you yore leg."

"I ain't quittin', mister. Soon as I git outta here I'm gonna git me a wooden leg and come gunnin' fer you again."

"Maybe I ought to save me some trouble and just shoot you right here and now," Charlie said angrily.

"You just go on ahead!" Amos shouted.

"Hey!" The doctor came in from the next room. "If you're going to aggravate my patient, I'll ask you to leave."

Charlie regretted losing control like that. "All right, Doc, I'm sorry. Maybe I'd better leave."

"You'd best git clear outta town," Amos said. "Ol' John Dougherty and his bunch is comin' up from the Creek Nation after you any time now. That's why I come on ahead, so's I'd have first crack at you."

Green interrupted. "Bunch? What do you mean by that?"

"John's got a gang put together," Amos said. "They been hittin' trains an' such, then holin' up near our place. I run errands and stuff fer 'em. That's how I heard they was comin' up here to git Charlie Martell fer Cimarron and Dandy Kilgallen."

Green laughed. "By God, Charlie! It appears to me that yore troubles is just startin'!"

111

chapter 10

Several evenings later Charlie returned to the boarding house after spending another frustrating day in town waiting to see if John Dougherty and his gang would show up. The cat-and-mouse game was made more irritating by Marshal Harry Green, who shadowed Charlie during his spare time.

As he hobbled up the porch steps he could hear the sound of loud talking in the parlor. There was a sudden silence as he went through the front door. Matty stood there with three of the railroad men who roomed there. The boarders looked sheepish as Charlie nodded a greeting.

"Howdy, Marshal Martell," one said.

"Howdy," Charlie said. Then he added lightly, "You havin' a meetin' or somthin'?"

"Well . . . in a way," the man answered. "I hope you don't take offense, but we was just tellin' Mrs. Koch that we're movin' out . . . on account o' . . . well, we know that they's some fellers gonna come gunnin' fer you and we figger . . . y'know . . . that we might git caught up in it . . . maybe hit by a stray bullet or somthin'."

Matty's voice shook with anger. "You just go ahead and move. But don't think on comin' back after this thing's been settled up."

"Now, Mrs. Koch . . ."

"They're right, Matty," Charlie interrupted. "I shoulda thought o' this myself. Ever'body here's in danger as long as I'm around."

"You ain't movin' out, Charlie!" Matty exclaimed. "If these jaspers want to go, then let 'em!"

"It's dangerous fer me too, Matty," Charlie said. "In fact, it's a good thing that Dougherty and his boys ain't showed up yet or they'd got me fer sure. I been keepin' reg'lar hours and a man under the gun cain't do that."

"We ain't takin' sides, Marshal Martell," the railroad man said, continuing to make excuses.

"I'm gonna have to camp outside o' town," Charlie said to Matty. "I'll change places ever'day or so. An' I'll come in irregular to eat too, if that's all right."

"You don't have to sleep in the open, Charlie," Matty said.

"I've been thinkin' about you, too," Charlie said gently. "It's no secret that Harry Green is a friend o' Dougherty an' he'll probably give him a hand in findin' me. If I stay here it'll be easy fer 'em to bushwhack me."

Matty recognized the logic of his thinking even if she didn't like it. "You do what's best, Charlie, but just remember to take all yore meals here." Then she turned to glare at the railroaders. "As for you, just git packin'!"

"If'n there ain't gonna be . . ."

"I said clear this property," Matty interjected. "I don't want no yeller bellies under my roof."

"There ain't no reason to call us that, Mrs. Koch."

"You'd better go, boys," Charlie said.

"Sure, Marshal Martell. So long. And good luck."

"Thanks." Charlie watched the three men

depart."I'd best git my gear throwed together."

"Yo're gonna have yore supper first," Matty said firmly. "There'll be extry helpin's since there'll be three empty chairs."

"Yo're lucky the other three haven't moved out," Charlie said. "I'm bad fer business."

"There's two other places in town to stay," Matty said confidently. "One is the hotel and the other is old lady Groggins' place. It's full o' fleas and her cookin' is enough to make a man swear off eatin'. As soon as her boarders hear I got three vacancies they'll be showin' up at my front door mighty quick."

During the evening meal, despite the ominous sight of Charlie's shotgun propped up on the wall near the table, Matty kept the conversation sparkling as her roomers took advantage of the extra food available. The hardworking men ate until they could barely pull themselves out of their chairs and waddle into the parlor for an after-supper smoke.

Charlie stood up and looked at Matty. "I'm gonna git my stuff ready and leave directly. It's best if I stay clear o' this place as much as possible."

"I hate seein' you do this, Charlie," Matty said. "But I'll be up to help as soon as the table's cleared."

Charlie stamped up the stairs to his room and pulled his gear from the small closet. There really wasn't much for him to do. After airing his bedroll when he returned from Arkansas he had rolled it up again. He picked this up and, since he was only taking the bare essentials and could obtain food and changes of clothing at the boarding house, the only other items he needed were his slicker in case it rained and his canteen. And to these his weapons and saddle, and he was fully equipped.

Matty came up with a paper-wrapped package tied

in string. "I got some biscuits here fer you to nibble on in case you git hungry before mornin'."

"Thanks, darlin'," Charlie said. He laid the food on the bed and held out his arms. Matty went to him and drew close to his lean body. He stroked her hair. "I don't like the idee o' bein' away from you, but it's best."

"I reckon I know it," Matty said with a sigh. "But I hate it just the same."

He kissed her, drawing her closer to him. She returned his lovemaking with a growing fervor until her breathing intensified to moaning pants. Suddenly she pushed away from him, her face flushed. She took a deep breath. "Oh, no, we don't! I'll bed with you and give in to yore husbandly rights anytime you want after we're married. Not before."

Charlie smiled down at her. "I don't think you ever looked pertier."

"Don't josh me, Charlie. I'm all tired out from a day's work and my hair's a mess."

"It's that look you got in yore eyes right now," Charlie said. "Makes you look right womanish and desirable." He reached for her again.

"Charlie!" She allowed herself to be swept up into his embrace once again, but she broke it off as she had moments before. "Not 'til we're man and wife."

He knew better than to try to change her mind. "Whatever you think's best, darlin'. I'd better go now. It really ain't a good idea fer me to spend a whole lot o' time here."

"When will I see you again?" she asked as they went down the stairs.

"I'll be comin' in irreg'lar so if Harry Green or anybody's watchin' they cain't pin me down to a routine," Charlie explained. "I don't want nobody to know exactly when I'll be comin' an' goin'."

"I wish I had some idea about when you might be showin' up," Matty said as they went out the back door toward the little corral. "That way I can be sure and have some hot meals ready fer you."

"Don't you go to no trouble now," Charlie said. "This ain't gonna last long."

"I pray not," she said.

Charlie saddled up his horse, then gave her a quick kiss before he swung up into the saddle. "I'm campin' down by them cottonwoods on Fall Creek tonight, but I'll be movin' around to differ'nt sides o' town. The trouble is that I need a place where anybody ridin' nearby cain't see me."

"You be careful, darlin'," she called as he rode out of the yard. "An' don't fergit to come in and eat."

"I won't, Matty," he called back. Then, with a final wave, he turned the horse toward the business district, riding with the shotgun in his left hand.

Ten minutes later he reined up in front of the marshal's office and slid from the saddle. Harry Green was lounging inside as Charlie limped in. The local lawman grinned at him. "Looks like Dougherty ain't showed up yet, huh?"

"I just want to tell you somethin', Harry," Charlie said menacingly. "An' you listen damned good."

"Why, hell, yes!" Green said sarcastically. "Yo're a U.S. marshal and I'm just a town officer. I'm always respectful to my betters."

"I ain't makin' lawman talk," Charlie said coldly. "I'm palaverin' man-to-man. And that could be worse fer you."

"I don't think so," Green said as his smiled faded.

"I ain't stayin' at Matty Koch's no more," Charlie said. Then he quickly added as the thought struck

117

him, "And I ain't takin' meals there no more either."

Green shrugged. "I don't give a damn one way or the other, Charlie. So why tell me?"

"Because I don't want you tippin' off yore friend Dougherty about my whereabouts when he comes sneakin' in," Charlie said.

"Let me tell you somethin' you obviously don't know," Green said. "Me and John Dougherty are far from bein' friends. Him an' me never did git along too good. So I ain't gonna tell him nothin'—*nothin'!* Got it? When you two sons o' bitches draw down on each other I'll just be around to pick up the pieces. But one way or the other I ain't takin' sides."

Charlie thought a moment. "If he bests me, are you gonna serve the warrant on him?"

"Hell, no! I may not like him, but we did ride together at one time. As long as he don't harm me or mine I'll let him go in peace."

"Yo're a rotten lawman," Charlie said.

"I'm a damn good one," Green said. "I got this town quieted down and under control. My only problem right now is bein' caused by you. Why cain't you wait fer Dougherty in Wichita?"

"Nolan Edgewater was gunned down here and he's gonna be avenged here," Charlie said. "An' that's that."

"I cain't run you outta town," Green acknowledged. "But by God, I don't have to play by any dumb set o' rules. I didn't with Nolan and I ain't with you. It's yore own doin' that a gang o' gunslicks is comin' fer you, and yo're the onliest feller that can change the situation."

"No I cain't," Charlie said.

"Well . . . maybe not," Green agreed reluctantly. "But I ain't gonna tell Dougherty nothin' about you."

Strangely, Charlie believed Harry Green at that moment. There was something in his voice and the expression on his face that reflcted truth in a straightforward manner. It was true that Harry Green seemed to be a good marshal for the town as well. Cowboys cutting up in the streets were quickly subdued and either arrested or turned out of Caldwell. And, among other things, the saloons were patrolled regularly and their noise and disturbances kept at a minimum. Charlie nodded. "I'll expect that from you, Harry."

"I'd appreciate it if you could keep the gunfight beyond the city limits," Harry Green said.

"Sorry. That's up to Dougherty now. If you don't tell him where I am I'll have to come lookin' fer him."

"You got a hell of a job cut out fer yoreself," Green said.

"Thanks fer the help," Charlie said sarcastically as he shuffled to the door.

"I noticed that bad hand o' yores got some color in it," Green remarked. "Is it gittin' better?"

Charlie held it up and showed him he could wiggle the index finger slightly. "Yeah, but I think I've took it as far as it can go."

"Too bad it ain't full recovered," Green said. "Yo're gonna be needin' it."

Charlie held the shotgun up. "This is better'n a right hand anytime." He went outside and unhitched his horse. After a careful look up and down the street, he pulled himself up into the saddle and rode out of town.

His first camp was in a pleasant spot beside the creek. The tall grove of trees there hid him completely from sight. And since he had no use for a fire, there would be no telltale smoke to give the little bivouac away. Even the horse had enough room to be comfortable and still remain hidden. Charlie unsaddled and hobbled the animal, then settled down at the base of a tree and relaxed. As darness fell he undid the bedroll and spread it out. He started to settle in when he remembered the biscuits that Matty had given him. He opened the package and pulled a couple out for a late snack to be washed down with water from the canteen. Then he stretched out and let his mind dwell pleasantly on the woman he had come to love.

He longed for her physically now and was capable of performing as a husband should. His reaction to her passion up in his room had proved that to him. But, as headstrong as she was, he knew he would have to wait until they were married. He closed his eyes, then moments later they popped open as he realized something.

He had never proposed marriage to Matty.

Charlie spent the next couple of nights in different places. The second camp was in a draw north of Caldwell. It seemed almost as good as the first area he chose, but a sudden prairie rain squall nearly flooded him out and he ended up soaking wet, having to abandon the place just past midnight to spend a miserable night shivering in wet clothing.

The next day, after changing into dry apparel, he took up his daylight routine of patrolling the town, especially the alleys and other areas that offered concealment to potential bushwhackers. Between these rounds he spent his time in the back of Will Johnson's General Store to relax and rest up from the exertion of the numerous tours.

The third evening he rode west five miles and simply slept out under the stars on the open plains. It was pleasant but the possibility of discovery made for a near-sleepless night as he awoke at every sound and change of wind.

He took his meal in the mid-afternoon on the fourth day. Matty planned his menus so that the food required only quick cooking or warming up while he changed clothes and bathed. He had never been one for regular, near-daily baths before but the hot soaks were so comforting he couldn't resist them.

"Ham and eggs," Matty said as he returned to the kitchen.

"Sounds good," he said. He would have kissed her but the maid was there.

Matty understood at once. "Harriet, you don't have to do the dishes now. The parlor wants dustin'."

"I'm halfway through," the maid said, continuing her task.

"I'll finish those," Matty offered. "You take care o' the parlor."

"Yes'm." She dried her hands on her apron and went out, mumbling something about a body should be left at work once it was started.

Matty sat in his lap and kissed him hard. "How'd you spend the night?"

"Perty good," he lied. "But I thought o' somethin'. It woulda been nice to have some coffee in my canteen. Maybe you could do that fer me."

"Sure, darlin'," she said. "But it'll git cold—unless you changed yore mind about makin' fires."

"I don't mind it cold," Charlie said. "It tastes perty good that way too."

"I'm surprised you didn't catch the grippe out

there."

"I been wet plenty o' times before," Charlie said.

"Well," she said as she got up. "You eat now and we'll talk later. Where you gonna spend tonight?"

Charlie grinned at her. It was just like a woman to speak of talking later, then launch immediately into conversation. "I thought it over and think I'll go back to that grove o' trees at the creek. It's as good a place as any, I reckon."

"When do you expect this here man to show up?" Matty asked. "Seems to me he ain't gonna make it."

Charlie ate pensively for several long moments. "That thought flitted across my mind too, honey. Maybe since I become a U.S. marshal he figures it'd be too risky fer him to come gunnin'. After Nolan Edgewater, he might not want to run the risk of all-out war bein' declared on him by the U.S. government."

"Oh, I pray so, Charlie!" Matty said enthusiastically. "Then maybe we can git on with our weddin' plans, darlin'."

"Uh . . . yeah, Matty," Charlie said, trying to think of a nice way to inquire into the origin of the idea of matrimony. "When . . ."

"On a Sunday afternoon," Matty said. "That's the best time fer a weddin'. It won't be nothin' elaborate, but I think Rev'rend Martin can organize a right nice service."

As she talked Charlie decided to abandon the idea of seeking out where the subject originated. He loved Matty Koch, he realized, and he wanted her. Actually she was the first woman he had ever really loved. There had been infatuations before, but these were shallow affairs brought on by the loneliness of his work and need for feminine company more than desire for any one particular woman.

He waited for her to pause in her happy chattering before he broke in. "I reckon if Dougherty ain't showed up in two more days we might as well set the date. I got to ride back to Fort Smith and check in with Judge Parker's court, then I'll be a free man . . . at least 'til the weddin'."

"Charlie! You act like yo're goin' to jail."

He wiped his mouth with the napkin and stood up to kiss her lightly on the cheek. "Only funnin'. I'd best git back to town in case somethin' happens," he said.

That day, like the others, turned into a boring routine of walking the alleys and sitting in the back of Johnson's store and whittling. By sunset he was settled back in the original camp, contentedly sipping on the canteen of coffee.

At that same moment, less than a hundred yards away, John Dougherty and four other gunmen gingerly skirted the far edge of Caldwell for a quick look at the town, before riding farther north to set up camp for the night.

chapter 11

Dawn had broken an hour before as Charlie gingerly rode into Caldwell. There were a few people on the street who scarcely gave him a second glance. They were aware of his situation, but it had been going on for so many days that by then it had become an expected thing to see Marshal Martell check on the town most carefully every morning.

Charlie made his rounds, then rode down the alley and hitched his horse in the back of Johnson's General Store. Willis Johnson, like the barber Sly Webster in Wichita, was an admirer of Charlie's and liked having him arond. There was a cracker barrel and a nice area for sitting and talking in the back of the establishment. Charlie spent all his time there between patrols.

"Coffee be ready in a minute," Willis said as Charlie came in the back door. The store owner was a tall, lanky ex-Rebel whose face was lined and seamed from the hard life of rural Alabama. He spoke in a soft drawl that contrasted sharply with the liveliness that sparkled in his green eyes. He kept the pot-bellied stove warmed up enough to perk up some brew despite the warm weather. He, like Charlie, was addicted to the drink and liked it hot, thick and plentiful.

"Seems like a nice day startin' up out there," Charlie said, sitting down. He tipped the chair back and propped his feet up on the woodbin.

"Gonna be a bit warmish, though," Willis said, slipping into the soiled white apron he used during business hours. "But, all in all, a perty decent bit o' weather."

Willis uncovered the goods on his counter and display tables, then opened the front door to announce his readiness for business should any potential client be around at that hour.

By the time the proprietor had completed his first routine of the morning, the coffee was good and hot. He and Charlie poured themselves each a cup, then settled back.

"I hear you an' Mrs. Koch is gittin' hitched," Willis remarked.

"Yeah."

"Congratulations."

"Thanks."

"When did you decide on that?" Willis asked.

Charlie shrugged. "I don't rightly know. It jest sorta come about somehow. You know how that goes."

"Yeah."

"If Dougherty don't show up in a coupla days I'm goin' back to Arkansas to turn in my badge," Charlie said.

"Yeah?"

"Yeah. Then we'll git married."

"Gonna stay on in Caldwell?"

"We been thinkin' on it," Charlie said. "The boardin' house ought to be enough to keep me occupied. There's always some totin' or mendin' to be done around the place."

126

"Ought to go into business," Willis advised him. "Since the Southern Cental come in, this place is really boomin'. Be bigger'n Wichita in another year or so."

"That right?"

"Sure as the sun rises in the mornin'," Willis said. "I expect to be doin' quite well. Even been plannin' on expandin' into the buildin' next door as soon as Tom Linker moves out. He's goin' up to Wellington. Big mistake. And I tole him, too. Jest 'cause it's the county seat don't mean Caldwell's gonna lag behind."

"Yo're prob'ly right," Charlie said agreeably.

Willis started to speak again when Baily Watkins, the clerk at the St. James Hotel, hurried through the store to the back. "Howdy," he said in an uneasy voice.

"What can I do fer you, Baily?" Willis asked.

"I want to see the marshal," Watkins said nervously.

"Sure," Charlie said.

"I thought somebody ought to tell you, marshal . . . I jest seen John Dougherty ride into town. He hitched up in front o' the Exchange Saloon."

Charlie tipped forward so quickly in his chair that he nearly spilled his coffee. "Was he alone?"

"Appeared to be."

A knot of apprehension appeared in Charlie's belly. He cleared his throat. "Obliged, Baily."

"Yo're welcome," the clerk said. He smiled slightly, then quickly left.

Willis' expression was stony with dread. "The moment's here, ain't it, Charlie?"

"Yeah." He finished the coffee and set the cup on the scarred table by the stove. "Reckon I'll go on over

127

to the Exchange and serve this here warrant I got."

"Go the back way," Willis said.

"Hell, yes, I'm goin' the back way," Charlie said testily. "You think I'm stupid or somethin'?"

Charlie, with the shotgun held securely in his good left hand, went through the back door and scuffled down the alley in a nervous gait until he reached the rear of the saloon. He paused and treated himself to several controlled deep breaths, then carefully tried the knob. It turned full and the door popped open from the release in pressure. Then Charlie pushed it away and stepped through with the shotgun leveled.

John Dougherty was the only customer in the place. The bartender looked surprised at Charlie standing there, then quickly understood what was taking place. "Goddam!" He backed away from the bar, then thought better of that and hurried around to the front. "Goddam!" he repeated, then scurried out the front door.

Dougherty looked over calmly. He was a tall, scruffy-looking man with light brown hair. A week's worth of beard growth decorated his face. "Howdy, Charlie. Long time no see. How you been?"

"I'm servin' a warrant on you, John. Issued by the federal court in Fort Smith."

"No shit, Charlie? I didn't know you was a lawman again," Dougherty lied. Then he grinned. "By God, it looks like you got the drop on me, don't it?"

"Slide yore pistol outta the holster—easy!" Charlie said forcefully. "And lay it on the bar."

"Sure thing, Charlie," Dougherty said. "Don't cut loose with that Greener, huh? Gittin' blowed in two would spoil my whole day."

128

"Now git yore hands up . . . high. We're goin' down to the marshal's office."

"Anything you say, Charlie," Dougherty said pleasantly. "Say! Is ol' Harry Green still the law here?"

Charlie didn't answer. "Take it easy goin' through them batwings, you sonofabitch. I owe you a load because of Nolan Edgewater."

As Charlie followed him he glanced at the pistol on the bar. It was an old one, badly rusted, with the look of being as dangerous to the shooter who used it as his intended victim. "You havin' a run o' bad luck?" Charlie asked as he stepped out onto the boardwalk in front of the saloon.

"Pure awful," Dougherty said in mock sorrow. "And now I been took into custody on top of it all."

Charlie caught the movement on the roof across the street just in time to hobble back a few quick steps. The shot struck one of the 4x4's holding up the wooden awning over the walk. As splinters flew, Dougherty made a quick dash around the corner of the building. Charlie started to shoot, but two old ladies stood in dumbfounded bewilderment in his line of fire. "Git off the streets!" Charlie hollered loudly. Then he repeated the command several times as he backed into the alley. The early morning shoppers and business people took his advice without a second's hesitation.

The street stood empty and quiet.

Charlie tried to sum up the situation. Dougherty had gotten free. He had a man on a roof across the street who could cover the whole area. The pistol he had surrendered so easily was probably some useless relic he had picked up somewhere. More than likely he was armed with his regular weapons now.

129

Going on the front side of the buildings was useless. The bushwhacker on the roof had a clear field of fire all the way over there. Charlie eased back to the rear of the stores and checked the alley. Then he stomped back down toward Willis Johnson's store.

Some instinct caused him a sudden uneasiness.

He didn't know if he had unconsciously seen or heard something, but the warning was just as real as if somebody had hollered in his ear. He pivoted on his good foot and found he had thrown down on a surprised pistolero who was just taking aim with a Colt Peacemaker. The Greener's double barrels flashed thunder and smoke, sending the ambusher careening off to one side with arms flailing. He collided with the wall of Tom Linker's leather shop, then collapsed back, leaving a large splash of blood on the building.

Without time to reload, Charlie pushed the shotgun in the crook of his right arm, and drew his pistol as he hurried back to Willis's.

Willis, armed with a Henry .44 carbine, stood back a ways from his front window. "There's a feller on the roof over there," he said. "He took a shot at you."

"Yeah, I know," Charlie said as he tried to catch his breath. "I need to git on top o' yore store to git at him, Willis."

"Sure thing, but be careful. If there's more of 'em, chances are they got another'n on the roofs on this side o' the street too."

"Damn! I hadn't thought o' that!"

"You can ease through the openin' in the roof at the rear," Willis suggested. "I'll keep you covered from the window. If that feller as much as raises his head I'll fire away."

"Thanks, Willis," Charlie said. He was sincerely grateful. It wasn't rare for the people of a frontier town to turn out armed in the event their bank was robbed or the town was threatened by armed cutthroats, but for Willis to step in and help out in a situation that most folks would consider of a personal nature was a unique gesture of friendship—and bravery.

The portal to the store's roof was reached with a ladder the proprietor kept handy. Charlie propped it up, then negotiated the rungs with some difficulty. Encumbered with a shotgun and a bad leg he was incredibly clumsy as he eased himself upward as best he could. When he reached the top he pushed the small door open carefully and peered out.

Willis had been right.

There was another gunman three buildings down on this side of the street. Charlie noted he could crawl across Willis' roof and onto Linker's since the stores were connected. But to reach the one nearest the potential ambusher he would have to jump across a narrow chasm between the structures. Even if Charlie could do it, the act would be dangerous as it would attract the henchman across the street.

Charlie eased out of the opening and laid out as flat and low as possible. Then, pressed closely to the roof, he negotiated the steep slant until he reached the top. A careful scan across the street showed the man there was looking the other way. Charlie pulled himself up and rolled down the other side to where the roof at Linker's shop began. Then he laboriously made his way up to the apex of that building.

He pulled the shotgun up and took careful aim. Even if the load spread it would send the would-be bushwhacker sprawling—perhaps even off the roof

131

and onto the street.

"Look out, Harry! He's down to yore right."

The voice carried across as the man on the other side finally spotted Charlie. His partner spun and fired a hasty shot that missed Charlie by five yards. Charlie blew off a load. His shells were for close-in work and they spread wide as the pellets flew through the space between the buildings and crossed over one, reaching the gunhawk's position. Both the shot and pieces of shingles were splattered into the outlaw. He howled in pain and grasped at his badly chewed face. Charlie pulled his pistol and steadied his aim as best he could while he fired.

The first and second shots missed as the intended victim staggered around blinded by blood, splinters and pellets. But the third caught him on an elbow and whipped him around. The wounded man stumbled back and fell off the building to the alley below.

Splinters from the roof then flew up around Charlie as the man across the street cut loose at him. Willis, down below, was as good as his word, and a few sharp reports from his Henry .44 made the sniper duck and withdraw from sight. Charlie hurried back as best he could, and nearly fell down the ladder as he lowered himself back into the store.

"Obliged, Willis," he said between breaths.

"Glad to lend a hand, Charlie," Willis said. "How many you got?"

"The one on the roof fell off and may still be alive, but from the way his face was cut up I figger he ain't worth much anyhow," Charlie said. "I got another in the alley before I got here. That's two. As far as I know there's only Dougherty and that sonofabitch across the street. But maybe there's more."

"That dumb bastard Baily Watkins said

Dougherty was alone," Willis said bitterly.

"Dougherty prob'ly made it look that way," Charlie said. "Them jaspers musta wandered into town one or two at a time."

"Too bad Dougherty knows the lay o' Caldwell so good," Willis said. "It appears he's got the place covered perty complete."

"I'm afraid he does," Charlie agreed. "But right now, from the way you made that other feller duck and take cover, he don't know exactly where I am. He has to figger I'm either here, in Linker's place or in the alley."

"Maybe you could . . ."

"Wait a minute!" Charlie exclaimed. "They had that one sonofabitch in the alley anyhow. If they don't know he's been hit, they might figger he could git me."

"You got a idee?" Willis asked.

"Not much o' one, but it might draw 'em back here," Charlie said. "You got a pistol handy? Then let me fire a coupla rounds back there, and you holler out the front fer Harry Green. Tell him that me and another feller are both down in the alley. If Dougherty or any of his men show up, I'll drop 'em."

"Yo're right. It *ain't* a very good idee, Charlie," Willis said plainly.

"It's either that or me sneakin' the streets and roofs again," Charlie said. "And I don't like the odds offered there."

"It's worth a try," Willis admitted. He went to his counter and brough back a Smith & Wesson .44. "Fire this one but be sure yore own is full loaded," he cautioned.

Charlie propped the shotgun by the door and took a careful look up and down the alley. Then he stepped out and began rapidly firing Willis's pistol in an effort to stimulate a surprised confrontation between two duelists. He hollered aloud a couple of times for effect.

Willis Johnson, at the front of the store, waited a couple of beats after Charlie finished, then yelled at the top of his voice. "Marshal Green! Marshal Green! Charlie Martell and another feller has shot theirselves in the alley behind my store. Marshal Green! Can you hear me? I think they're both dead."

There was no answer as Charlie stood back from the doorway. He listened intently, hoping that no curious townspeople would make an unexpected appearance in the middle of the alley. Suddenly he heard boots scuffling and the sounds of two men talking excitedly as they neared the site.

"I don't see nobody," a voice said.

"There's some feller layin' in the alley down a ways," the second man said. "By God, that looks like ol' Pete, don't it?"

"It's him. But where's that goddammed marshal?"

Charlie stepped out. "Here, you sonofabitch!" The first barrel hit the nearest man in the crotch, turning his genital area into pulverized meat. As he spun to the ground, the second blast splattered into his partner's chest and neck, somersaulting him over a stack of crates and barrels.

"Hold it, Martell, God damn you!"

Charlie, holding the empty shotgun, turned to find John Dougherty had thrown down on him with a Smith & Wesson .44-.40. "There was five of you," Charlie said more to himself than to Dougherty.

"Sure was," Dougherty said, grinning. "And yo're a dead man, Charlie Martell."

"Hold it!" Marshal Harry Green's voice was sharp

134

and clear as he stepped around the side of the building.

Dougherty nodded to him. "Howdy, Harry. Yo're jest in time to watch me send Charlie to hell fer what he done to Dandy and Cimarron."

"Drop that gun," Green said to Dougherty. "I ain't foolin', John. *Drop it!*"

"You starpackin' sonofabitch!" Dougherty hissed. He swung the pistol and fired. Harry Green backstepped under the force of the slug's impact but managed to shoot twice. Dougherty received hits in the head and belly, then collapsed at Charlie's feet.

"Jesus, Harry!" Charlie said, surprised.

Harry Green grimaced and stumbled forward a few steps before falling to the alley dirt. Willis Johnson glanced out the door and wasted no time. "I'll git the doc."

Charlie sat down beside Green. The lawman clutched at the wound in his chest. "Surprised . . . I showed up . . . Charlie?"

"I reckon." Several people made an appearance now that the shooting was obviously over. Charlie beckoned to them. "Three o' you fellers git ahold o' the marshal here. One at his shoulders, one at his feet and, you there, support his middle. I want to git him up to the doc's right now."

The men did as they were told and met Willis and Doctor Hubble on their way to the scene. The physician retraced his steps back to his upstairs office as the men bearing their injured burden followed as rapidly as possible. Charlie limped up the stairs after the little procession as the streets filled with the morbidly curious people of the town.

Harry Green was laid on the operating table as Doctor Hubble made everyone but Charlie leave.

135

"What made you jump in on my side?" Charlie asked.

Harry Green's face was wan and drawn. "Yo're a bad influence . . . Charlie," he said with a weak grin. "Ever since . . . you got back . . . from Arkansas . . . I been thinkin' . . . that yo're really . . . one hell of a man . . . here you was all . . . crippled up . . . but you done proud . . . in avengin' . . . Nolan Edgewater."

"That's enough talking," Doctor Hubble said.

Green shakily raised a restraining arm. "Lemme . . . tell Charlie . . . somethin' afore . . . you start . . . probin' . . . Doc . . ."

Hubble took a hurried glance at his patient and knew that there was nothing he could do for him anyway. He smiled. "Sure, Marshal. You're in good enough shape to wait awhile. Don't worry. Go ahead and talk with your friend."

Green grinned with an effort. "I never . . . figgered somebody . . . would call . . . us . . . friends, Charlie."

"Me either," Charlie said.

"Well . . . you shamed me, Charlie Martell . . . you was more'n a damned . . . fine man . . . you showed me what . . . this here . . . star on my chest . . . really stood for . . ." He paused and drew a labored breath as waves of pain built up and subsided. Then he turned back to Charlie. "That . . . bastard Dougherty called . . . me a starpacker . . . I liked that . . ." There was another break in his conversation before he could speak again. "I . . . run a . . . clean . . . town . . . here, Charlie Martell . . . I realized while . . . you was facin' Dougherty alone . . . that Caldwell had . . . suddenly got dirty . . . and it was . . . my fault . . . I had to be . . . a lawman and

136

". . . do my duty . . . like you . . . was doin' . . . and I done it . . ." Green eyes suddenly glazed over and half closed.

Doctor Hubble examined him closely. "Well, he's gone."

"My God!" Amos Gleason stood in the door of the bedroom supported by his crutches and one leg. "I never seen things in this light before."

"How you doin', kid?" Charlie asked.

The young Indian ignored the question. "I seen you a couple o' times during the fight down there," he said to Charlie. "You was right brave, Marshal. I admire the way you stood up to all of 'em."

"You'd be better off if you modeled your life after Charlie Martell than John Dougherty and his ilk," Doctor Hubble said. "And get back into bed!"

"Yes, sir," Amos said, still looking at Charlie with unrestrained admiration.

"Charlie!" Matty rushed through the door and charged into him, grasping tightly with her slim arms. She looked up with tears streaming down her face. "Oh, Charlie!"

"I'm fine, darlin'," Charlie said, squeezing her with his good arm. "Not a scratch."

"I thank the Lord," she said, regaining her composure. "Truly I do."

"Let's go home," Charlie said. "I'm suddenly weak in the knees." They walked from the office and down the stairs. The crowd had gathered up the five dead outlaws and were propping the bodies up on planks for the photographer who had appeared with his clumsy camera at almost the exact moment the final shot was fired.

"Hey, Marshal Martell," the photographer called. "Will you kindly consent to pose with the dead

137

men?"

Charlie nodded and walked over to the corpses. The man who had fallen from the roof obviously died from a broken neck. The others who died from the shotgun were bloodied and messy, while John Dougherty, his dead eyes opened as wide in surprise as they had been at the sight of Harry Green throwing down on him, was the most natural. Charlie stood beside the gang leader as grinning townspeople supported the planks holding the other bodies. He patiently went through three posings before he walked back to Matty.

"Y'all better git to findin' a new city marshal," he said to the crowd. "Harry Green died doin' his duty."

"He *helped* you?" Matty asked incredulously.

"I'll explain over a cup o' coffee," Charlie said. He spotted Willis Jonhson and waved to him. "Many thanks, Willis, I appreciate what you done."

"Don't mention it, Charlie," the store proprietor said. Then he went inside to continue his business day.

Charlie and Matty walked arm-in-arm back to the boarding house. He smiled at her. "I jest got one more thing to do. A ride to Fort Smith and turn in a death certificate on John Dougherty and . . . this." He pointed to his U.S. deputy marshal badge.

"Don't you tarry down there in Arkansas," Matty warned him in good humor.

"With the pertiest gal in Kansas waitin' fer me?" Charlie remarked. "Not likely, ma'am, not likely a'tall!"

chapter 12

Fort Smith was crowded as Charlie rode across the bridge that spanned the Arkansas River. There was a festive mood as farmers, cowboys, and other frontier types milled about, enjoying the good mood of the place. Children, laughing and shouting, scampered through the throng as their exasperated mothers vainly tried to maintain some sort of control over them. Charlie had to rein in and swerve his horse several times to avoid collisions wth the kids—or some staggering drunk who had yet to catch the attention of the local law.

He dismounted in front of the courthouse and took one disinterested glance at a mournful prisoner who stared lethargically from the cellar jail. Heck Thomas was at his desk with his feet propped up. His rugged face folded into a delighted grin as Charlie walked in. "Hello, Marshal Martell!" he boomed in jocular formality. "Glad to see yo're back."

"You git my wire?" Charlie asked as he shook hands with the other lawman.

"We did," Heck said. "You got the death certificate fer John Dougherty?"

Charlie fished around in his pockets and brought out the document. He unfolded it and handed it over. "Signed and sealed by the coroner of Sumner

County, Kansas," he said.

"Well, sir, you got a bonus comin'," Heck said, examining the document. "Two dollars fer doin' in Dougherty—you'd git the same if you arrested him, but a killin' pays like puttin' him into custody."

"I understand I got expenses comin', too," Charlie said.

"You betcha, Charlie. The U.S. of A. gov'ment is gonna pay you ten cents a day fer the time you was trackin' that man down. 'Course we got to submit the papers on it first." Heck laid the death certificate carefully on the desk after working some of the creases out. "Now! You ready fer another manhunt, Charlie?"

"No, thanks," Charlie said. "I'm turnin' in my badge, Heck. I'm gittin' hitched."

"No!" Thomas offered a hand in congratulations. "Who's the lucky lady, Charlie?"

"She's a widder woman in Caldwell," Charlie said. "Name o' Matty Koch—she comes from Missouri. Got a boardin' house."

"That's fine news," Heck said. "I'm always glad to see one o' the boys settlin' down. What kind o' work you goin' into?"

"We figgered there'd be a few things around the boardin' house to tend to," Charlie said.

Heck pulled a sheet of paper out of one of the desk drawers and handed it, along with a pen and ink bottle, to Charlie. "Write out yore resignation, Charlie, and I'll turn it in to Judge Parker along with this death certificate. We ought to git the papers drawed up for yore expenses too. Lemme think . . ." He stared at the ceiling as he tried to mentally calculate what Charlie had coming to him. "Seems you'll have more'n two dollars there. Where do you want it

140

sent?"

"Care o' the Merchants and Drovers Bank in Caldwell, I reckon," Charlie said. "Might as well send along my salary there too. What about the government horse the judge let me use? Where do I turn it in?"

"You can keep it," Heck said. "We wrote it off a while back. Consider the animal one o' the side benefits o' this job—though the Lord knows there ain't many."

Charlie sat down and began to carefully write. He stopped to look at the badge he had just pulled from his shirt. "Had to see how to spell 'deputy' and 'marshal,' " he said sheepishly.

Heck laughed aloud. "Yeah, most o' the fellers do. But we all know how to spell 'U.S.,' don't we?"

Charlie grinned and resumed his task. He printed large capital letters with his left hand, doing the job slowly and laboriously so the message might be easily read. When he finished he handed it to Heck. The lawman perused it carefully.

> June the 5th, 1881
> Fort Smith, Arkinsaw

Judge Parker
Fedral Cort
Fort Smith, Arkinsaw

Deer Yore Honur,
   I respecfuly quit as U.S. Deputy Marshal.
      Yores trulie,
      C.H. Martell

"That'll do her, Charlie," Heck said. "Wait a bit while I take it to the Judge and let him know yo're here."

"Say, before you go," Charlie said. "What's the crowds here for? There's some kind o' celebration?"

"Tomorrow's hangin' day," Heck said. "Matter o' fact, one o' the pris'ners is Cimarron Gleason. He's due to meet his Maker with three other fellers."

Charlie walked out to the porch and looked over in the direction of the gallows that were partially hidden behind the high fence. A twelve-inch thick oak beam ran the length of the structure and was capable of hanging up to twelve men at one time. As Charlie stood there a man stepped through the fence and slowly walked toward him. The stranger was a heavily bearded thin man who moved in a slow gait. As he drew near he nodded politely to Charlie.

"Howdy," Charlie said as the man passed. Just then Heck Thomas came out on the porch.

"Know who that is?" Heck asked.

"Nope. But there's somethin' kinda eerie about him," Charlie said.

"That's Charles Maledon—our hangman," Heck said. "He was prob'ly checkin' the gallows out fer tomorrow."

"That's somethin' I don't think I could do," Charlie said. "I've shot other fellers, but to cold bloodily step up and slip a noose over a man's head—particular if he ain't done nothin' personal to me—is more'n I could stand."

Heck nodded in agreement. "That's why we have use fer men like Maledon."

"Even his name sounds like somethin' bad," Charlie said.

"Yeah. Judge Parker wants to see you, Charlie," Heck said. "Cmon, I'll take you in."

Charlie followed the other into the judge's chambers. Isaac Parker stood up and offered his hand along with a friendly smile. "I am most sorry to be losing your services, Mister Martell. But allow me to offer felicitations on your coming nuptials."

"Sir?" Charlie asked as he shook hands with the judge.

"Congratulations on your marriage," Judge Parker said.

"Oh! Thank you kindly, yore Honor," Charlie said.

The judge invited him to sit down, then did the same himself. "I understand there were four other men with John Dougherty. Were they identified?"

"Yes, sir," Charlie said. "But I don't think this here court knowed any of 'em. They was Texans and hadn't been in the Injun country very long."

"You may have single-handedly destroyed a gang of this region's worst desperados," the judge said.

"I had some help from Harry Green," Charlie said. "Fact o' the matter is it was him that shot Dougherty after he had the drop on me."

"I'm surprised to hear that," Judge Parker said. "As I recall you expected very little assistance from Mister Green because of his friendship with Dougherty."

"Yes, sir," Charlie said. "But it turned out they wasn't real good friends anyhow. And I reckon that Harry took a likin' to bein' a lawman and felt like he had to help me."

The judge nodded. "Most commendable. You men who enforce the law here in these wild territories are certainly not remunerated in a manner to match your devotion to duty. I have written countless times to Washington imploring them to raise your rates of pay and compensation in order to attract and retain the best of men. We are losing you, Mister Matell, and possibly Heck Thomas someday as well."

Hec laughed. "Not me, yore Honor. I was borned and bred to be a lawman. I'll live and die as one, I reckon."

"Then I shall let you inspire me to perform as best I can at my own task in this tangle of law enforcement," Judge Parker said. "And I must be doing a good job—I understand that I am now being referred to as 'Hanging Judge' Parker."

"Yes, sir," Charlie said. "Beggin' yore pardon."

"There has been no place in the history of man like the Indian Territory when it comes to lawlessness," Judge Parker said. "White renegades who are immune to prosecution by the Indian tribes run rampant out there or use the area to hide and rest up between committing the most heinous of crimes in other parts of the country. When any of them are dragged out of there by a marshal of this court and found guilty of a capital offense he will *hang!* We must enforce justice to the utmost of our abilities and I could not do less, as I realize how deputy marshals in the jurisdiction have given up their lives in pursuing the high goal of establishing peace and security in the area. Your very good friend Nolan Edgewater is a commendable example of a man giving his life in the service of bettering this world for mankind."

"A lawman don't mind riskin' his life if he knows the court'll back him up to the hilt and really throw the book at varmints he turns in," Heck Thomas said.

"Yes, sir," Charlie echoed.

"And that philosophy is the backbone of an effective system of justice," Judge Parker said. "Now, if you'll excuse me, I must get back to this brief."

"Goodbye, sir," Charlie said, shaking hands again. "I hope to see you again sometime."

Charlie and Heck went back to the porch. "When you headin' back to Kansas?" Heck asked.

"I was figgerin' on a early start tomorrow," Charlie replied.

"Why don't you stick around and watch the hangin'?" Heck asked. "After all, one of the condemned men was brung in by you."

Charlie thought about what the judge had said about seeing justice done all the way through. Maybe it would be a good thing to see one of his last acts involving the law brought to a final conclusion. "Yeah. I think I'll stay and watch ol' Cimarron dance at the end o' yore hangman's rope. I reckon my obligation to Nolan Edgewater will be really complete then."

"Fine, Charlie. Want to bunk here in the courthouse? We got a back room jest fer that."

"Jake with me," Charlie said. "I'm gonna board my horse, then git somethin' to eat."

"Don't stuff yoreself," Heck said. "The U.S. of A. ain't feedin' you now."

"Never was a generous provider," Charlie said with a laugh as he shuffled down the porch steps.

Charlie pushed his way through the crowd the next morning and only with some difficulty managed to reach the porch steps and ascend them. Heck Thomas stood there and eyed the growing crowd with nods to acquaintances and admirers. He turned to Charlie. "Mornin'. How was breakfast?"

"Not bad," Charlie said. "Lot cheaper'n in Wichita or Caldwell even. When do the festivities start?"

145

"Perty soon. Let's git on down there to the gallows yard before this mob really thickens up."

With the more able-bodied Heck leading the way, Charlie clumped after him. Once inside the fence it was evident that Charles Maledon, the hangman, was well prepared to begin the most important activities of the day.

After a quarter of an hour there was a sudden hush in the throng. This was immediately followed by a surge in noise as the four condemned men were escorted from the basement jail to their place of execution by a team of deputy marshals. As they walked through the gate Cimarron Gleason was the last man. He caught sight of Charlie and smiled slightly. "Be a good day fer you," the Creek Indian said.

"A worser one fer you," Charlie replied stonily.

The prisoners, all bearing restraining chains and cuffs, slowly mounted the thirteen steps to the platform. Each was accompanied by a marshal to one of the nooses hanging from the thick beam running the length of the scaffold.

The final lawman who followed the solemn procession carried several sets of papers in his hands. He stepped forward and raised his hand in a quieting gesture. Within two minutes the only sound was the buzzing of insects and an occasional cough in the crowd. In a dull, monotonous voice he read the death sentence of the first prisoner.

The condemned men stood silent and grim as their individual dooms were put into legal phraseology. The first was Dutchy Krause, described as a white and not an Indian, age 28, who met an itinerant peddler named Ellsworth Morgan traveling through the Choctaw Nation. He joined the man and accompanied him for several days. Krause showed

146

up alone at the town of Cache Bottom with Morgan's wagon and goods which he attempted to sell. The local Indian law became suspicious and investigated the matter. Morgan's body was found submerged with rocks in a creek some twenty miles away. Krause was turned over to a U.S. deputy marshal for transport to Fort Smith and trial.

Lucas Meal, Negro and not an Indian, age 23, had been invoved in a card game at a cattle camp in the northern part of the Indian Territory near the Kansas line. Meal lost five dollars and stalked angrily from the camp after an argument with a Texas cowboy named Big Red Girard. Later, after becoming intoxicated, he returned to the card game and without warning shot and killed Girard. He fled but was tracked down and captured by other members of the cattle outfit, then taken to Judge Parker's court for trial.

Thomas Mally, white and not an Indian, age 32, while traveling through the Seminole Nation stopped at the ranch of Danny Mark. He was granted a meal and permission to spend the night. Shortly after midnight he appeared in the bedroom of Mister and Mrs. Mark armed with a pistol. He ordered the husband out of the house with threats of death and pistol shots. Then he committed rape upon the wife several times. When Mister Mark returned with several neighbors they found Malloy dead drunk under the kitchen table. Only the unexpected appearance of U.S. Deputy Marshal Heck Thomas prevented a lynching the next day. The prisoner was brought to the Federal Court of the Western District of Arkansas where he was found guilty and sentenced to hang.

Cimarron Gleason, a Creek Indian, age 27, shot

and killed Norbert Singleton, a white man and railroad baggage car clerk, during a robbery perpetrated on a train of the Missouri-Kansas-Texas Line near Caddo in the Choctaw Nation. He was apprehended by Mister Charles H. Martell, a private citizen, in Muskogee of the Creek Nation and turned in to federal marshals at Fort Smith, Arkansas.

Each disclosure of the prisoner's crimes brought shouts from the crowd as they vented their fury verbally on representatives of the class of men who made their existence a living hell.

"At this point," the marshal droned, "the condemned will be allowed a few last words." He pointed to Dutchy Krause.

Krause, visibly trembling, shook his head as his eyes rolled in terror. The crowd hooted his cowardliness as his agitation increased.

"You pissin' in yore pants, are ya, Krause?" somebody yelled from the crowd.

"Lucas Meal," the marshal announced.

The black man stepped forward, emotionally under control. His voice was deep and resounding. "I got myse'f into trouble on account o' gamblin' and whiskey. Let dat be a lesson fer you young jacks out dere. Dey hangin' me today fer a crime I don't even remember doin'—but good honest cowboys said I done it—so I'll own up to it."

He was given a round of applause as he stepped back to stand in front of the noose that would end his life.

"Thomas Malloy."

"Yez is woise'n animals yeselves," Mallow spat in a New York accent. "Fer weeks yez is locked me up in a goddammed basement that is filthier'n anyt'ing I ever seen in me whole life. Yez ain't woith . . ."

148

The final part of his oration was drowned out by catcalls and shouts of derision.

"Cimarron Gleason," the lawman said.

"I broke the laws of Injuns and white," Gleason admitted. "Maybe I'm sorry and maybe I ain't, but I can die like a Injun. You'll see that perty quick." He turned to Charles Maledon, who stood off to one side. "C'mon and do yore work, you wicked old man. I'm as anxious to git outta this life as these damn people are fer me to go!"

This was followed by a combination of applause and shouts of hatred at the defiant young Indian. It took the presiding marshal several minutes to bring the crowd under control. "Now, Rev'rend Arthur Fellow of the Presbyterian Church of Fort Smith will offer up a prayer. Kindly remove yore hats and bow yore heads, if you please," he said with exaggerated politeness.

The clergyman, a thin, solemn middle-aged man, who had stood unnoticed off to one side now took the center of attention. He raised both hands, with one holding a Bible, as he looked upward as if he wished to beseech the Almighty face-to-face.

"Dear Lord, these good people are gathered on a sad occasion this day as they send the spirits of four sinners to your tender mercy. We beg in Christian charity that your divine compassion will lift the terrible burdens borne by these tortured souls and make their time in eternity as light as possible . . ."

"*Bullshit!*" a loud voice exploded in the crowd. "We want them sonso'bitches to burn in hell ferever!"

". . . The true driving force of Christiantity is *forgiveness*," the preacher continued as he shot a withering glance toward the crowd. "And, as we forgive them in our humble mortal way, we do pray that . . ."

"Let them bastards see if the souls o' their victims show any forgiveness," another crowd member shouted.

". . . *We do pray that* You, too, will find heavenly clemency possible for them. We ask this in Jesus' name. Amen." He lowered his gaze and his hands, then addressed the crowd directly. "Let us sing *Rock of Ages.*" He began the hymn alone but within a few moments the crowd took up the words.

Charlie, his gaze riveted with all the hate in his being on the killer of Nolan Edgewater, finally checked the scene around him. The men about to die stood bound and shackled on the scaffold attended by the marshals as their potential killer, Maledon, waited patiently. The gentle, beseeching words of the religious song filled the arena of death as the macabre ceremony began drawing to its terrible conclusion.

The singing ended and the minister walked from the scaffold. The marshals stepped forward and blindfolded each of the prisoners before setting the black hoods over their heads. Then Maledon went to each man and adjusted the handwoven nooses made of Kentucky hemp just right. The knot had to be under the left ear just behind the jawbone in order for the fall to produce instantaneous death by breaking the neck cleanly and quickly.

Utter silence permeated the arena now. Even the birds had stopped singing for those terribly long last seconds. A loud creak exploded as the trap was sprung and the four bodies dropped to the full extension of the ropes.

Krause and Gleason were still after only two or

three minor twitchings. Lucas Meal's legs drew up for several seconds before straightening out in death. From the contortions of his body it was obvious that the rapist Malloy was strangling to death. The knot had slipped out of position during the fall.

The crowd applauded and whistled in approval.

Charlie spent a second night in Fort Smith since the hangings took place so late in the morning. By dawn of the next day he was saddled and packed at the livery. He rode into the main street with every intention of crossing the Arkansas and heading back to Kansas, but he felt he had one more bit of business before leaving. After asking the directions of several persons he finally arrived at the house he was looking for. He dismounted and hitched his horse and walked through the front gate. His knock on the door produced the appearance of a sad-faced woman in her thirties. Charlie took off his hat. "Mrs. Edgewater?"

"Yes, sir."

"My name is Charlie Martell. I was a good friend o' Nolan's."

She smiled and opened the door. "Please come in, Mister Martell. Nolan spoke of you many times. My name is Mary." The Edgewater house was disorderly with boxes and crates. "I'm movin' back to Tennessee," she said. "Gonna live with my brother there. His young'uns is up and growed, so there'll be plenty o' room."

"That's nice, ma'am," Charlie said. "I'm on my way back to Kansas and I wanted a chance to meet you. The last o' Nolan's killers is gone now."

"I know," she said, leading him to the kitchen in the rear for the coffee she knew he craved from the

151

way Nolan had described him to her. "Even if Cimarron Gleason was convicted fer another feller's murder."

"I reckon it's all the same, ain't it?" he asked.

"Yes," she said. "And Nolan's still gone."

He sensed the emptiness now, almost the uselessness of the whole quest for vengeance, but still he had to admit it had all been necessary. "But think how we'd feel right now if Gleason and his bunch was still runnin' around free and loose."

"I reckon yo're right. When somebody does a terrible wrong there ain't no peace 'til the price is full paid," Mrs. Edgewater said. As she served his coffee she noted the empty spot on his shirt. "Where's yore badge, Mister Martell?"

"I quit and turned it in," he said. Then he smiled. "I'm gittin' married up in Caldwell . . . widder lady."

She sat down in surprise. "Why, that's plumb wonderful! And yo're givin' up bein' a lawman too?"

"I reckon," Charlie said.

"She won't have to worry 'bout bein' a widder again," Mrs. Edgewater said. "Leastways not 'til yo're old and gray."

"Yeah," Charlie said as he sipped the hot coffee.

She sighed aloud. "I don't know why y'all do it. All that danger, the low pay and not even a 'thank you kindly' from the folks you helped. Here you are all crippled up and Nolan dead . . . and fer what? The law . . . the awful, terrible *law!*"

He knew he couldn't explain it to her since he didn't understand it all himself. He quickly finished the coffee. "I got to go, Mrs. Edgewater. Goodbye."

"I'll walk you to the fence," she offered. They wound their way through the clutter and out of the house. As he went through the gate she allowed him a little wave. "I was proud meetin' you, Mister Martell. I wish you the best."

"Thank you kindly," Charlie said.

"Have a nice trip now," she said, watching him get up into the saddle in his peculiar clumsy manner.

"I'll do my best," he smiled. "If yo're ever in Caldwell look us up."

"Mister Martell," Mary Edgewter said with conviction, "I ain't never steppin' foot west o' the Mississippi again!"

chapter 13

The reddening sun was just beginning to set and a cooling breeze wafted off the prairie as Charlie rode up to the corral of the boarding house. He lifted himself free of the saddle and slid to the ground weary and stiff from the long ride. His bad leg felt like needles were being driven into it as he pulled the gate open. He limped badly as he led the horse into the enclosure.

Minutes later Matty ran out to meet him as he scuffled stiffly across the yard to the house. The sight of her smiling face washed away the fatigue of the trip in an instant. He held out his arms. "Hello, Matty, my love."

"I'm so glad yo're back, darlin'!" she said, wrapping her slim arms tightly around him. She held up her face for a kiss and accepted it happily. "Supper's almost ready."

"I reckon I could do with a bite," he allowed as they walked up to the house. "How's ever'thing been while I was gone?"

"Perty quiet," she said. "There was some newspaper men and such around to find out about the big gunfight, but they're all gone now. One feller was down all the way from Kansas City."

"I ain't surprised," Charlie said. "It's quite a story

155

havin' five fellers come into a town with killin' on their minds."

"That Willis Johnson is so modest," Matty said. She walked through the back door as he held it open for her. "He claims he didn't do nothin' to help at all."

"He did enough," Charlie said as they walked into the kitchen. "And I'll allow as how Harry Green did too."

"There was a nice funeral fer him," Matty said. "He woulda been proud."

"That's good. They got a new city marshal yet?"

"No. Some o' the men in town take turns. As quiet as things have been there ain't been no pressin' need. Just the usual loud drunks, that's all." She joined the hired girl in preparing to take the food to the dining room. "Go on in and sit down. We'll be eatin' directly."

Charlie went into the dining room, then stopped at the unexpected sight of the Indian boy, Amos Gleason. He was seated with a stranger among the boarders at the table. The youngster smiled shyly and stood up. "Howdy, Marshal Martell." He offered his hand.

Charlie uneasily took it, then nodded to the stranger who sat beside Amos.

"This here is Mister Willard, my school teacher from the Creek Nation," Amos explained.

"How do you do, Marshal," Willard said.

"I'm a plain ol' mister now," Charlie said, taking a chair. "Turned in my badge at Fort Smith." He shook hands with Ned Orson, the printer on the *Caldwell Post.* "You save me a copy o' the write-up on the shootout?"

"Sure did, Mister Martell," Orson said. "Got three

156

as a matter o' fact."

"Obliged," Charlie said.

"Well?" Amos stood there, still wearing a slight grin.

"Well, what?" Charlie asked testily.

"Ain't you noticed? I'm standin' up." Amos walked stiffly around the table to display a brand new peg leg, the leather padding on the bottom barely scuffed. "I'm still a little sore, but gittin' used to it."

"That's good," Charlie said. "By the way, you livin' here?"

"Yes, sir," Amos said, going back to his chair. "Got me a job and ever'thing right here in Caldwell."

"He's a smart boy," Orson said. "I managed to secure him a spot on the paper as a printer's devil. He'll be learning a good trade that will provide well for him and any future family."

Willard the school teacher smiled at Charlie. "You probably don't realize what a good influence you've been on this lad, Mister Martell. He was always one of my better students until he fell under the spell of his cousin, Cimarron Gleason. When he saw you face the dangers of . . ."

"They hung Cimarron," Charlie interrupted. "I seen it myself in Fort Smith."

Amos' expression saddened a little. "I always liked my cousin—and ol' John Dougherty too—but when I seen they wasn't good as you one-on-one, I reckon I did some deep thinkin' on 'em, Mister Martell. They didn't stack up to you a bit."

"It's a shame that tragedy was necessary to straighten the boy out," Willard said. "But at least the deaths of certain men have brought about some-

157

thing good."

"I miss my leg," Amos admitted. "But if you can be one hell of a man like you are, then there ain't no reason I cain't git what I want outta life, too."

Charlie remembered his days as a hopeless drunk in Wichita and was suddenly glad that young Amos would not have to go through that. It would be doubly hard for an Indian. "Nice to hear you found a good job," Charlie said sincerely.

Willard sighed. "I just fervently hope and pray that Mister Orson and the other printers can do more about his grammar than I ever could."

"Don't worry," Orson said. "The boy spells very well and has his punctuation down correctly. We'll influence him with a few bawling outs, but in the end he'll be a finished journeyman printer."

"I'm thinkin' about goin' back to the Creek Nation later on and openin' up my own paper," Amos said brightly.

"Here we go!" Matty and the maid came into the room with steaming trays of food. The hungry boarders dove into the meal with a will and the talking died out altogether as they consumed the repast in a bout of serious eating.

Desert was a peach cobbler with a thick sugared and cinnamoned crust that was literally destroyed by the hungry diners. The supper ended with the final clinks of forks being laid on plates as the last sips of coffee were slurped. As usual they sat in silence as if contemplating the pleasant sensations they had just enjoyed as well as the comfort of filled bellies.

"Thank I'll have a cigar," Orson, the printer, said. He slowly got up and ambled out to the front porch as the others followed. Charlie remained seated.

158

Matty came into the room and saw him still sitting there. "You want somethin' else, darlin'?"

Charlie rubbed his throbbing leg. "Not here," he said. "But a long hot soak'd be a pure pleasure, believe me."

Matty kissed his cheek. "Sure enough, sugar. You go on upstairs and I'll heat up some water."

"I'll do the totin'," Charlie said, dreading the thought of negotiating the stairs several times with buckets of water. But he knew how hard it was for Marry or her maid to perform the task.

"Maybe if we asked one o' . . ."

"I said I'll do it," Charlie said. "You just heat 'em up, honey."

Three-quarters of an hour later Charlie was stripped and standing by a steaming tub. He lowered himself into the water as he grew used to the heat until he was seated up to his neck in the soothing comfort of the bath.

Matty came in with some thick clean towels. "How you feelin', darlin'?"

"Perty good and gittin' better," Charlie said.

"I reckon yo're awful stiff and sore from that long ride up from Arkansas, ain't you?" she asked. "You been tendin' to that hand?"

"Ain't had much of a chance," Charlie said.

"Charlie!"

"Well, darlin', it's kinda hard to take care o' somethin' like that when yo're campin' out or sleepin' in the marshals' quarters in the court house."

"Well, don't worry none," Matty said. "Later on we'll give that hand a good rub and have some coffee and a long talk. How's that sound?"

"Real good, darlin'," Charlie said. He made a sud-

159

den grab for her, but she managed to work free just in time to push his head under the water. He surfaced sputtering and spitting hot soapy suds.

She laughed out loud. "I tole you I'm a Christian woman and won't be dallied with, Sir."

He grinned at her in good humor. "Yes, Ma'am. I'm sorry, Ma'am. You ain't mad, are you, Ma'am?"

"I certainly am," she said, still smiling. "You jest sit there and keep yore head filled with good pure thoughts. Can you do that?"

"I reckon, Ma'am," Charlie said. He waved her a farewell as she left the room, then closed his eyes and dozed contentedly as the balminess of the bath eased his distress.

Charlie stayed in the water until it was lukewarm. By then it was dark outside and most of the roomers had retired for the night. After toweling himself dry he donned the clean clothes Matty had laid out for him. Then he clumped down the stairs to the kitchen.

Matty was there alone shelling peas for the next day's supper. She stopped her task as he sat down to fetch him a cup of coffee. Then she turned her attention to his hand.

"How long has Amos been here?" he asked.

"Less'n a week," Matty replied. "He's a real nice boy, Charlie. His school teacher says he goes to church reg'lar and was a right smart student in school. Doctor Hubble has got to where the thinks a lot of him, too. Says he spent quite a bit o' time talkin' with him and says Amos is one o' the brightest youngsters he's come across in quite a spell. I reckon he wants to help him out, too."

"Yeah," Charlie said. He watched in silence as Matty massaged and manipulated color in to the hand. "At least the kid has a good job."

"Yes," Matty said. "Mister Orson says he's doin' fine at the paper."

"In a way he's a better feller than me," Charlie said. "I'm gittin' married in a coupla days . . . and instead of a real job I'm movin' into my wife's business . . . which was built up with her dead husband's money."

"Don't you talk like that, Charlie," Matty said. "That's the silliest thing I ever heard of."

"But it's true," Charlie said. "Sorta like I was sittin' around his house drinkin' his likker."

"Has any o' the other men said anything to you like that?" Matty said.

"No," Charlie admitted. "Nobody's said nothin'. It's jest my own thoughts, that's all."

"You put such nonsense right outta you're mind," Matty urged him.

"I'll try," Charlie said. But he knew the situation would gnaw at him from the minute he married Matty and moved into her room.

The street around the Methodist Church was clustered with buggys, surreys, heavy farm wagons and other vehicles as well as horses hitched to anything sturdy enough to hold them.

When a noted gunfighter gets married it is an event unusual enough for the locals to forget such social protocol as invitations and to dress up in their Sunday-go-to-meetin' best to attend the ceremony. The one propriety observed, however, was that those with bona fide, engraved "invites" had first choice at the pews before the rest of the throng swarmed in and settled themselves inside the wooden building as best they could.

161

It was hot and stifling as the ladies fanned themselves and the men swatted at the flies that buzzed through the congregation in tight circling spirals. High, tight collars and wool suits were the order of the day and heavy perspiration soaked through the garments until they were wilted and soaked. But nobody seemed to mind as they breathlessly waited for the appearance of the bride.

Charlie, with his best man, Willis Johnson, stood by the altar with Reverend Martin. The three men were relatively cool in comparison with the packed crowd only a few feet away. Wide open windows let a slight breeze, cooled by the heavy foliage of the trees outside, dance over them in periodic breaths of activity. The organist, Willis' wife, June, kept glancing down the aisle for her cue of Matty's appearance to begin the wedding march. Willis himself walked down to the front door for a look-see and returned with a shrug of his shoulders.

"Maybe she changed her mind, Charlie," he said with a grin.

"It'd show how smart she really is," Charlie quipped back.

"A bride's preparation is long and complicated, Mister Martell," Reverend Martin said. "And I do hope I shall see you attending services here with your new wife. She never misses a Sunday."

"I'll sure try, Rev'rend," Charlie said without conviction. On an impulse he turned to Willis. "I fergot to ask if you had the ring."

Willis pulled it out of his pocket. "Here she be."

"Put it back!" June Willis whispered loudly to her husband. "You'll drop it and we'll all be down on our hands and knees lookin' fer it when Matty shows up."

Willis winked at Charlie and slipped the ring back into his pocket. "See what yo're in for, Charlie? Anything you do from now on is gonna be scrutinized and looked over worser than any sergeant in the army."

June suddenly straightened up and the first notes of the famous song burst forth in a high-pitched melody. Heads craned to look as Matty, with Doctor Hubble giving her away, made an appearance at the door.

She was dressed in a new, light-blue satin dress with a modest bustle of the same color. Her hat was a simple lace affair with a light veil that fell loosely across her face. Matty's wedding bouquet was made up of Kansas sunflowers wrapped in pale blue tissue and held together with bright yellow bows made from a wide ribbon.

Charlie though her absolutely beautiful at that moment.

Her slim body moved with an easy grace—rather than the hurried movements she used in the kitchen—and, as she came down the aisle, all her feminine charms seemed multiplied tenfold. Even her hands, generally rough and red, seemed lily-white and dainty as they gently held the flowers in front. Charlie, smiling shyly, took her arm from the doctor and they both turned to face Reverend Martin.

Charlie was mesmerized by his woman's bloom of beauty and scarcely heard the words of the ceremony as intoned by the preacher. Only after the vows had been completed and he had slipped the ring on her finger did he fully become aware of their surroundings.

"You may kiss the bride," Reverend Martin stated.

Charlie lifted the veil—as he had been instructed to do—and, observing the propriety of the times, kissed her lightly on the cheek. Then, arm-in-arm, the couple turned and walked down the aisle.

The men now whooped in frontier style as they shouted their congratulations while the women, mostly teary-eyed, smiled their best wishes with gentle expressions of affection.

Willis' son Judson held the buckboard steady as Charlie helped Matty up into the seat. They had to wait for Willis and June to join them, then Charlie flicked the reins and they rode off to the business district amidst the renewed shouts of wishes for long life and happiness.

The first stop was the photographer's studio for the official wedding portraits. The cameraman, who had not long ago callously photoed the corpses of John Dougherty and his gang, now bustled around and arranged several poses to record the happy day in decorum and good taste.

There were photos of the bride and groom; bride and Doctor Hubble; groom and best man; preacher, bride and groom; and other arrangements until over two hours had passed before they once again trooped outside and the group made its way to the boarding house for the reception.

The wedding meal was roasted buffalo steaks. Amos Gleason had supervised the cooking using the Creek manner which combined both white and Indian methods of preparation and seasoning. The animals had been butchered, dressed out and wrapped in wet burlap for burial under coals and dirt since the day Charlie had returned from Fort Smith. During the ceremony the main course had been dug up and final work done so that now, cut up and waiting in caldrons, it was ready for the hungry throng that was expected. There was roast corn, potatoes and plenty of beans along with barrels of whiskey and beer for the crowd of several hundred—most of whom weren't invited but were expected anwyay—although there were certain amenities to be observed before the party proper could begin.

The first step was the cutting of the wedding cake. This, like the pews in church, was only for invited guests but everyone was expected to observe the event. The large confection was carried out to a table set up in the back yard next to the buffalo meat. Charlie took the large knife and cut two pieces. He handed one to Matty and he took the second. Then they each fed a bite to each other as the crowd applauded.

Then Willis Johnson, along with several other local musicians, made an appearance. The storekeeper motioned for quiet and announced, "The first dance as selected by the bride will be *Beautiful Dreamer.*" There was complete silence as the little ensemble prepared themselves, then, with the beginning of the music, Charlie led Matty to an empty area cleared for the dancing. He slipped his lame arm around her, took her hand and gently waltzed through the melody (played slower than usual out of consideration for his leg) for several moments. After the expected and obligatory round of clapping, other dancers joined them and the festivities began in earnest.

The wedding party was a huge success. There were fourteen separate fist fights and one minor brawl that involved a half dozen of the town's wilder drinkers. Willis Johnson and his musicians were so drunk by midnight that they were finishing songs as much as sixty seconds apart. Two or three times they started up with two different songs before they realized the error and stopped while the crowd roared in amusement and delight before the little band swayed and staggered back into a semblance of organization.

A little past two the festivities wound down. The younger unmarried gallants had retired to the saloons in town to finish up their drunkenness with the soiled doves, while family men gathered their broods to begin the dark trek back to ranches and farms. Charlie and Matty sat at the table that bore the remnants of the wedding cake, holding hands as the last of the revelers made their goodbyes.

"Gonna be a big mess to clean up in the mornin'," Matty said, observing the debris in the pale yellow glare of kerosene lanterns.

"Well, darlin', you got a husband to worry about such things now," Charlie said. "I'll douse them lights, else the wind's gonna blow one over and burn the whole town down."

"Before you clean up this mess tomorrow you move yore things into my, er . . . *our* room," Matty said.

"That I'll do," Charlie said as he walked around the yard, blowing out the flames in the lamps. He came back and took her hand. Silently they walked to the house. After stepping over Orson, the printer, who was passed out in the kitchen, they went upstairs and down the hall to her bedroom, the farthest and biggest one.

Inside she slipped her arms around him. "You glad about what you done, Charlie?"

"I sure am, honey," he said sincerely. He kissed her gently, then more aggressively as she responded without restraint, letting her passions free themselves from the moral fence she had built around them.

"Oh, Charlie, love!" she said as she broke off the kiss. "I'm yore wife now."

And Charles Houston Martell, who had regained part of his manhood with a gun, now completed the reclamation of his maleness in a gentler way.

chapter 14

That summer of 1881 surrendered gracefully over
southern Kansas while autumn, taking the tranquil
hint, eased in languidly as it cooled and colored the
prairie country with gently dropping temperatures.
The frigid, howling winds of winter were still far
over the northern horizon despite the shortening
days and cooler air.

Charlie Martell stepped through the gate of the
newly constructed chicken yard and hobbled among
the feathered inhabitants to the coop. A board had
come loose on the back side—noted by Matty—and he
had come to fix it—goaded by Matty—before the
opening proved too much of a temptation for a neighborhood dog or fox off the prairie—as envisioned by
Matty.

He shoved the board in place and hammered it
with a few clumsy blows. He was able now to grasp
objects with his right hand, but the permanently
bent elbow still made it difficult to manipulate
things perfectly or efficiently. Still, it felt good to actually put the hand to use.

"Charlie!" Matty hailed him from the house.

"Yes, honey?" He walked back through the gate
and carefully fastened it shut.

"We'll be needin' water in the kitchen."

"I'll tend to it directly," Charlie shouted back.

"We need it now, darlin'," she sang out.

" *Goddammit!* " he swore.

"What was that, honey? I didn't hear you."

"I said 'goddammit,' " he yelled. "*God damn it!* You hear me that time?"

Matty came out onto the back steps. "What're you swearin' like that for?"

"Because I'm gonna put the hammer and nails away before I git that water," Charlie said angrily. "You wait a minute, hear?"

"We got to have the water fer coffee and to boil the potatoes fer supper," Matty said patiently. "And don't fergit them Websters is comin' down from Wichita fer a visit. They'll be here jest shortly before it's time to eat."

Charlie took the hammer and nails to the tool house he had built by the corral. Only then did he go to the well and draw two pails of water. He kept a pad of old rags wrapped around one handle. This he carried in the weaker and more sensitive right hand. When he had first toted water with it, he had been only able to maintain a grip on a quarter of a bucket, but now he had worked himself up to half-full. In another couple of months he figured on being able to manage two full pails at a time.

He stumped into the kitchen and set the water on the counter. "Y'all gonna need more'n this?"

Matty's face was rigid with indignity. "I think not, Mister Martell. *Thank you very much!*"

" *Yo're very welcome,* " Charlie said. "Anything else you got in mind to nag about, or can I git back to my reg'lar work?"

Matty turned to the maid. "Excuse us fer a minute." She waited for the grinning girl to leave the kitchen before she pivoted to face Charlie with both hands on her hips. "Now jest what's got into you, Charles Houston Martell?"

"I wish to hell you'd plan yore work out so's you don't have to keep hollerin' at me ever' fifteen minutes," Charlie said. "Damn wimmen! Run around like chickens with their heads chopped off."

"There are many things that must be done in the proper runnin' of a boardin' house," Matty said. "If they don't pop up in a nice orderly way to suit you, then that's too bad. But they're things that got to be tended to—and right away."

"I swear, Matty, you could turn a train wreck into somethin' worse," Charlie said.

"Then I'll jest sit myself down and you tell me and the girl ever' little move we got to make," Matty said. "A big, strong, smart man like you shouldn't mind ridin' herd on a coupla doty females. You can make all the decisions from now on."

He ignored the invitation. "I'm gittin' back to my paintin' on the front porch—which I musta started and stopped at least a dozen times today." He limped into the dining room and sent the maid scurrying back into the kitchen with a curt motion of his head. The paint on the porch still awaited him. He stirred it angrily for several moments, then stopped. He sighed loudly then got back up and shuffled through the house to the kitchen.

"Excuse us fer a minute," he told the hired girl. Then he watched Matty for several moments as she angrily plopped the peeled potatoes into a pot on the stove. He scratched his head self-consciously. "I'm sorry."

Matty stopped her work and turned around. "We're silly, that's what we are."

171

"I don't know what's the matter with me," Charlie said disgustedly. "I know these things got to be done when they pop up. I guess I jest ain't used to this sort o' . . . well, this mendin' and fixin' and totin'. I feel like I was doin' chores again on my pa's ranch in Texas."

"I shoulda took in consideration that this is somethin' kinda new to you, darlin'," Matty said. "Yo're so much help."

"Even if I'm a grumpy bear?" he asked, smiling.

She walked over to him and slipped her arms around him. "Yo're such a *nice* grumpy ol' bear."

He kissed her. "I'll put the paint up and git ready to go to the depot fer the Websters. I should be back up here with 'em in time to settle 'em in and be ready fer supper."

"All right, darlin'," Matty said.

Charlie went back to the dining room. "You can go back now," he told the maid.

"Good Lord!" the girl exclaimed. "Why can't you two make up in the bedroom like other folks?"

Sly Webster and his wife, Alma, were given the empty room at the upstairs back of the house for their visit. The Wichita barber wasted no time in informing the boarders of his long friendship with Charlie.

"Yeah, I knowed Charlie here fer quite a few years now," Sly told them. "Back when he was a marshal in Wichita even."

"Yes, indeed," Alma echoed. "He used to be a reg'lar guest at our house. And we do miss him so now."

Charlie smiled slightly, remembering the conversation he had heard between Sly and his wife when

172

Alma had absolutely forbade the crippled ex-lawman to ever set foot in her home again. Still, he had enjoyed her cooking on occasion and Sly's hospitality had been sincere and warm. He could offer the two of them no less. "You both showed me a great deal o' kindness," he said.

"I notice yo're puttin' on weight, Charlie," Sly said with a wide grin. "Looks like this here married life is agreein' with you."

"I like it perty good, I reckon," Charlie admitted.

"I'm afraid he's somewhat bored, though," Matty said. "There ain't much excitement in runnin' a boardin' house."

"Not like a shootout, hey, Charlie?" Sly asked.

"It's kinda quiet and routine," Charlie said.

"I see yo're usin' that right hand," Sly said turning serious. "Looks dang near normal, don't it, Alma?"

Alma forced herself to take a quick look at the maimed claw that had always disgusted her, then she stared in unabashed wonder. "It *is* normal! You been to a doctor, Charlie?"

"Nope," he said. "Looky here." He wiggle all the fingers with the exception of the little one. "I'm gittin' more'n more strength in it ever'day thanks to Matty. She was the one that started workin' with it. But it looks like the pinky jest won't respond no matter how much rubbin' and soakin' it gits."

"Reckon you'll be holdin' a gun with it soon?" Sly asked.

"I ain't tried, bu since my elbow is set solid bent I don't think it'd do me much good."

"You'd have to shoot from the hip," Sly said, making a pseudo draw with his hand in demonstration.

"I don't figger I'll be usin' a gun again 'cept fer

huntin'," Charlie said.

The other boarders were by now feeling left out and, one by one, they made their excuses and left the table. After they were gone Alma patted Matty's hand. "You'll have to git Charlie to bring you up to Wichita. It's growin' by leaps and bounds."

"Willis Johnson says that Caldwell's gonna be bigger'n Wichita someday," Charlie said. "Population in this town tripled when the Southern Central and Fort Scott built their terminus here."

"The railroad ain't gonna be that important without cattle," Sly said. "And with the way the farmers is takin' over this part o' the country, the only range left is gonna be around Dodge City. Now, there's a place that *might* be bigger'n Wichita some day."

There was a sudden scuffling of booted feet at the door and several men, led by Willis Johnson, entered the dining room. "Howdy," Willis said.

Matty was surprised to see the townspeople. "Evenin'. Can I git you some coffee?"

"No, thanks, Matty," Willis said. "I don't want to waste a lot o' time 'cause there ain't none."

"What's goin' on?" Charlie asked.

"Paul Simpson is down at the marshal's office drunker'n a lord," Willis said. "He cain't even git to his feet hardly."

Charlie laughed. "Some marshal."

"We want you to take his job, Charlie," Willis said bluntly. "Seventy-five dollars a month and one dollar for each arrest."

"Well . . ." Charlie looked over at Matty.

Matty briefly considered Charlie's chafing at the boarding house chores. She knew in her heart he was bored stiff and unhappy with the uninteresting work. But she still had misgivings and doubts. "This

174

ain't like bein' a U.S. marshal, is it?"

"No, Matty," Willis answered. "He'll jest keep the peace here in Caldwell, that's all."

Sly Webster was excited. "By God, Charlie, what do you think o' that? You'd be walkin' tall as a starpacker in yore own town."

"You wouldn't be travelin' around the country?" Matty asked.

"Only fer short trips to pick up or deliver a pris'ner," Charlie explained. "Not runnin' all over the country constantly like them fellers outta Judge Parker's court."

"Thank the Lord!" Matty said with a sigh. "Charles Houston Martell—take the job!"

City Marshal Charlie Martell wasted no time the next morning and at an early hour was busy in his office checking the paperwork of the previous lawman. It was badly lacking in completeness, neatness and accuracy, so the old veteran tackled that task first.

Even the routine correspondence had to be brought up to date. Letters from other law enforcement agencies, government bureaus and private citizens had to be answered, noted and filed in the records. A good part of his first hours on duty were spent on this job and it would have been worse if Amos Gleason hadn't gotten permission from the *Post* to spend the day helping him.

Next was the proper recording of arrests and fines. It appeared that quite a case could be built up against the drunken Simpson for embezzlement since there hadn't been a fine put down in the book for the previous three weeks. The police judge's own documents could be used as evidence against the ex-marshal, but Charlie thought it best to let it simply be forgotten.

It was early evening before all was in proper order. Charlie and Amos both closed the final books and shoved the last papers into the file with deep breaths of relief. "Let's go git some supper," Charlie said. "Then I can tend to my late patrollin' along with other business."

"I'm hungry and that's a fact," Amos said eagerly.

"I appreciate yore help," Charlie said. He scrawled a note with his clumsy right hand and stuck it on the glass in the door.

Gone to the bording house. Back soon.

C.H. Martell
City Marshall

Matty was just serving as he and Amos made their entrance. The railroad men looked up long enough to make polite salutations before they turned their eager attention back to the meal. Orson, the printer, was more amicable. "How'd the work go?" he asked.

"It was a chore," Amos replied. "I didn't realize how much correspondence and filing goes on in a city jailhouse. I just figgered they tossed a feller inside and that was that."

"You through fer the day?" Matty asked.

"No, dear," Charlie said. "Night is my busiest time. I got to check things out and prob'ly drag in a drunk or two. I should be home around three in the mornin'. If ther's any arrests, I got to be down in the office to bring the pris'ners before the judge. After them cases is settled I can come on back home fer a few hours."

176

"How long are you gonna keep this up without a deputy?" Matty asked. "Yo're puttin' in some mighty long hours, Charlie."

"Harry Green done the job alone," Charlie said.

"He was a bachelor and his comin' and goin' at odd hours didn't upset no household," Matty countered.

"Willis said they was gonna hire somebody jest as soon as the right man showed up," Charlie assured her. "Don't worry none about it."

"Well, as long as yo're happy with the work, I'm happy with it," Matty said.

"I do feel good about it," Charlie said. "But I'm figgerin' on droppin' by the house now and then fer coffee. It'd sure be nice if a pot full was always waitin'."

"It will be," Matty promised. "Don't you fret about that."

Charlie ate hurriedly, then ran a napkin across his mouth as he stood up. "I got some more business to attend to. See y'all later."

"G'night, Marshal," Amos said.

Matty walked him to the front door and kissed him on the cheek. "You be careful, hear?"

"Sure will," he said. Then he clumped down the front steps and headed for the business district. But instead of going directly to his office he turned down the street to the nearest saloon.

Business was still slow, with only a few drinkers at the bar while a card game was going on in the rear. The proprietor, a large red-nosed man named Sweeney, waved to Charlie. "Hiya, Marshal. Care fer a drink?"

"I'm here on business," Charlie said. "Send the girls down to my office."

"Wait a minute," Sweeney said. "We made a deal

with Simpson."

"Simpson ain't marshal no more," Charlie said. "I am. Git them gals down there pronto."

"Goddammit, Marshal . . ."

Charlie's face paled in anger. "If you give me any guff, Sweeney, I'll close you up so quick yore head'll spin. I said I want the wimmen that work fer you to be down at my office and I mean *now!*"

Sweeney swallowed hard. "Sure, Marshal, I didn't mean nothin'. I'll send 'em down this minute."

Charlie called on the rest of the town's saloons before turning back to his headquarters. By the time he got there, a couple of dozen of the town's soiled doves stood inside waiting for him.

"Evenin', ladies," Charlie said politely. "In case there's some o' you that don't know me, my name is Charlie Martell and I'm the new marshal o' Caldwell." He pulled his court book from his drawer and opened it to the first empty page. "Now choose the names y'all are gonna use from now on 'cause I don't want you changin' 'em on me. It musses up my records. The fine's five dollars cash money, same as always. Line up and plead yore cases, please."

The girls, smiling and jostling each other good naturedly, did as they were told. A combination of sweat, whiskey and cheap perfume filled the office as the girls waited their turns. They were rough-looking, unrefined young females. Many were already showing the stark results of their profession. Alcoholism and illness made their eyes harder and faces grimmer than their youth should have allowed. Each stepped up with a plea of guilty, then laid out five dollars. Charlie duly wrote in each name and fine.

This practice was in essence not a punishment, but

178

actually the purchase of the right to practice prostitution in the city limits of Caldwell, Kansas. While whoring was illegal, it was recognized as a necessary part of the community's economy. The cowboys, buffalo hunters and other frontiersmen who frequented the saloons also spent money in the legitimate enterprises of the town. That and the fines paid by these women kept commerce at a comfortable level in the town.

And Charlie Martell, as city marshal, had his place in this lucrative practice that would provide street lamps, drinking fountains, boardwalks and other benefits for the citizens—all earned in the cribs behind the saloons by girls known, among other names, as Big Alice, Hard Ass Kate or Happy Mary.

chapter 15

The nights were now cool enough that the small fire in the office stove was comfortable. Charlie and his new deputy marshal, Zach McKay, kept a pot of strong coffee in a perpetual boil on the cast iron implement.

McKay was a youngster up from Texas with a little experience as deputy sheriff in a sparsely populated county in the south of that state. He had little to say, did a commendable job and seemed to anticipate his chief's wishes, as well as having that special instinct for applying the right amount of lawful authority each situation warranted. He and Charlie got along fine.

On a quiet weekday evening as they sipped coffee in silence each was lost in his own thoughts. Their seperate reveries were interrupted by the sound of shots down the street.

"Damn!" Charlie said. "It's my turn to go out, ain't it?"

McKay grinned and took another drink from his cup. "It sure is, Marshal. Have fun."

"Thanks," Charlie said with a wink. He left the office and walked down the street where the portly barkeep of the Exchange Saloon met him on his way to the office.

"Some damn buffalo hunter's tryin' to shoot up the place," the man complained. "Sonofabitch ain't hit nobody yet, but he's so goddammed drunk he don't know what he's doin'."

"You shouldn't've sold him so much rotgut," Charlie said as he rapidly scuffled down the boardwalk.

"Hell, he was already three sheets to the wind when he come in," the bartender said defensively.

Charlie stepped through the batwings and saw the hunter hanging onto the bar at the far end of the room. His eyes were glazed and half-closed as he waved his pistol around. He finally noticed that everyone else in the place—who had crowded over to one corner of the saloon—was looking toward the door. He whirled drunkenly and spotted Charlie. "Who th' hell are you?"

"Town marshal," Charlie said, easing his pistol from the holster. "Yo're under arrest."

The drunk started to say something, then he hesitated as his alcohol-soaked mind suddenly remembered a certain fact about Caldwell. "Uh . . . wait a minute . . . are you Martell?"

"I am," Charlie said.

"Shit!" He quickly laid his pistol on the bar and stepped back with his hands raised. "I ain't shootin' it out with you, Marshal. I heerd 'bout you clean down to Texas."

"Let's take a walk down to the jailhouse then," Charlie said.

"Any goddam thing you want," the hunter said, staggering toward the door. He stopped and stood swaying in front of Charlie. "It's a honor and privilege to be arrested by you, Marshal Martell," he slurred drunkenly.

Charlie grabbed his prisoner by the collar and propelled the clumsy reveler down to the jail.

The one thing he didn't notice was the four young cowboys who took a sudden interest in him. During the short time Charlie was in the saloon, each sized him up and studied him carefully, then huddled together in hushed but animated conversation after he left.

Meanwhile, Charlie pushed the drunk through the door of the office, then he and McKay subjected the prisoner to a quick search. The man had eighteen dollars, some loose bullets for both pistol and buffalo rifle, along with an ivory-handled pen knife.

"Where's the rest o' yore property?" Charlie asked.

"Down at the liv'ry with my hoss and mules," the man said. "I was havin' one last celebration afore I went out to the hunt. Winter's comin' and them buffalo are gonna have a real growth of fuzz on 'em in a coupla months."

"Well, yore celebratin' is over now," Charlie said. "You'll sleep it off and go before the police judge in the mornin'."

The hunter went peacefully into a cell. "Much of a fine, Marshal?"

"Prob'ly two dollars," Charlie said. "You didn't resist arrest."

"Now with *you!*" the man said. He scowled at McKay. "But if you'd showed up, I'd've kicked yore ass up under yore hat, kid."

McKay, who hadn't locked the door yet, pulled it open and stepped into the cell. He slammed a hard punch into the hunter's face. As the prisoner's buttocks hit the floor he was treated with a heavy kick to the chest that toppled him over on his back. The

183

drunk sighed loudly, then passed out. The young lawman slammed the bars shut and turned the key.

"Yo're gonna have to learn not to take things so personal," Charlie said. "A lawman gits talked down to a lot."

"That don't mean I've a mind to stand fer it," McKay said.

"You'll develop a thick skin," Charlie said. "Reckon I'll go on home now. I don't think you'll be too busy tonight."

"Me either," McKay said. Since the younger man had been hired as deputy, they had split up the long hours necessary to police the town. While both worked late on Saturdays, they took turns going off duty on quieter nights.

"I wouldn't bother stayin' past midnight," Charlie said as he went to the door. "See you tomorrow."

"Sure thing, Charlie. Good night."

Charlie rattled a few doorknobs on the stores he passed until he reached the street that led to the boarding house. Then he stuck his hands in his pockets and leisurely strolled home.

Some twenty yards behind him, the four cowboys from the Exchange Saloon skillfully kept to the shadows as they followed the lawman through the moonlit neighborhood.

When Charlie arrived home he went straight to the kitchen, where he knew Matty would be waiting with a late snack. He kissed her cheek and pulled off his coat. "How you doin', love?"

"Fine," she said. "I got some o' that beef pie warmed up fer you." She dished out a generous helping and set it in front of him.

"Damn!" he said patting his belly. "Ever'body's remarkin' on how I'm puttin' on weight. And no won-

184

der, from the way you feed me."

"That lean look don't flatter a man yore age, Charlie," Matty said sitting down beside him. "You should git portly. Makes you look more of a success."

"Hell, Willis Johnson is one o' the most successful businessmen in Caldwell and he's skinny as a rail."

"You said 'damn' and 'hell' already in jest the first few minutes you been home," Matty said.

"Sorry, honey," he said digging into the pie.

"You promised not to swear in the house anymore," Matty reminded him.

"I'll watch it," he said. He stuck his spoon in the thick gravied meat again, then stopped. He listened intently.

"What's the matter?" Matty asked.

"Shhhh!" He strained his ears, then slowly got to his feet and drew his Colt. He opened the back door as quietly as possible and eased through. A couple of minutes later he came back to the table and started eating again.

"Somethin' out there?" Matty asked.

"Prob'ly a cat," he said between bites. "I thought I heard somethin'."

"Put the dish on the counter when yo're finished," Matty said. "I'm turnin' in."

"Sure, darlin'. G'night."

"G'night." She kissed him and sleepily left him alone in the kitchen.

After Charlie finished he took care of the bowl as Matty had asked. Then he turned the kerosene lamp down and carried it with him as he went toward the stairs.

The shadow suddenly appeared out of the parlor before he could react.

The brilliance of the first shot fully illuminated

185

the room for a millisecond. Charlie shifted the lamp to his right hand as the second bullet shattered plaster and wood beside his head. Then he drew and quickly fired twice. The figure jumped straight up then staggered forward a few steps before falling in the pale light.

Charlie sat the lantern on a nearby table and took a step before the ear-splitting shot from the kitchen exploded. Something heavy struck his chest and he was slammed across the fallen body to the floor. He rolled over and saw a cowboy approaching him with a drawn gun.

Another loud shot split the silence and the man's chest opened up in an explosion of crimson. Charlie stuck up his good foot to ward off the falling body.

Matty stood on the stairs with the .44 Winchester carbine. "I tole you the wimmen in my family ain't shrinkin' violets," she said as she cocked the handle and chambered another round.

"I believe *that!*" Charlie said as he felt his chest. There was no blood, but he noted he was sore as hell as he got to his feet. The sound of running attracted his attention and he hobbled quickly out the front door. "Hold it!"

Two men crossing the front yard suddenly stopped and threw up their hands. Neighbors ran up with guns and threw down on the duo as others awakened by the shots appeared on the scene.

"Charlie!" Matty called. "Drag these two jaspers outta the house. They're bleedin' all over ever'thing."

"We'll take care of it, Marshal," one of the neighbors said. "C'mon, Morris." The two men went inside the house and directly reappeared with the bodies of the two men. After dumping the corpses out on

186

the street they returned to Charlie.

The two prisoners were boys in their late teens. They trembled with fear as the murderous looks of the townspeople bored into them.

Amos Gleason didn't have time to slip on his peg leg and was on crutches when he came out to the yard. When he saw the prisoners he was amazed. "Bob Duncan and George Malone!"

"You know 'em?" Charlie asked.

"Sure. They're from down my way." The Indian looked over the two bloody bodies lying in an undignified heap. "But these fellers is strangers to me. Who are they?"

"Elmer Torrey and Phil Dougherty," one of the young captives said. He turned to Charlie. "We didn't do nothin', sir. We was jest watchin',"

"Dougherty? Not kin to John Dougherty?" Charlie asked.

"Yes, sir," the boy said. "Phil was his kid brother."

"Goddammit!" Charlie swore. "How many more of em is there?"

"That's all," the kid said. "There was another brother but he got drug by a horse and killed."

"What about their father?" Charlie asked as visions of countless Doughertys coming to Caldwell gunning for him danced through his head.

"He's a preacher man, Marshal," Amos interjected. "And perty old anyhow. John tole me about im awhile back."

"That's a relief," Charlie said as Deputy Marshal Zach McKay trotted up.

"I was jest leavin' the office when I heard the shootin'," he said.

"Cuff 'em and take 'em down to the jail," Charlie

187

said. "Then see to the two dead 'uns. I'll be down directly."

"Sure thing, Marshal," McKay said. "Hey, how about a coupla you fellers helpin' me?"

The two young men were roughed up and pummeled as they were put in the restraints before being pushed and kicked down the street to the marshal's office.

"I reckon it's over," Charlie said as he walked back to the house.

"Look at the mess," Matty complained as she came in. "Them two shot holes in the wall and then bled all over the carpet." She noticed Charlie holding his chest. "They didn't shoot you, did they?"

"Naw," he said. "But I did git hit. Bring the lamp over." The only damage he suffered was a bruised chest. The marshal's star had taken a glancing blow from the bullet and obviously deflected it away. The metal was dented and bent.

"That badge saved your life, Charlie," Matty marveled.

"It was a indirect hit, but coulda hurt me serious," Charlie admitted. "I'm sore as hell." He sat down in one of the parlor chairs as the roomers trooped back into the house.

"Anybody fer coffee?" Matty asked.

"Since we're up, why not?" Orson the printer remarked.

"I'm gonna go put on my leg," Amos said.

In less than a half hour the kitchen was crowded with boarders and restless neighbors as the shooting incident blossomed into a minor social event. Everyone marveled at Charlie's badge as he sipped the fresh hot brew.

A few cups more and Matty was serving snacks of

bread and cold meat. The people, normally of a most modest persuasion, chatted easily as they stood and sat around in their bathrobes and dressing gowns. The festivities were interrupted by a local bartender who burst in on the scene.

"Marshal! There's a bunch down at the jail wantin' to lynch them kid cowboys. McKay sent me to say he's havin' a hell of a time."

Charlie wasted no time in securing his gun and hurrying out of the house after the barkeep. When he arrived at the jail he found a crowd of fifty drunken townspeople gathered on the boardwalk. McKay was having a shouting match with three of them as the others joined in from time to time with threats. Charlie pushed his way through the throng and joined his deputy. The crowd quieted and backed away a little.

"Let's break it up," Charlie said. "There'll be no lynchin' in Caldwell."

"They're part o' that damn Dougherty bunch, ain't they?" someone asked. "We're gonna learn 'em to stay outta our town once and fer all."

"I ain't gonna spend a lot o' time on this," Charlie said as he drew his pistol. "You got a minute to git the hell outta here or I'm gonna start shootin'."

"Hell, it was you they tried to kill!" a man in the crowd reminded him.

"And I'm satisfied to let the law deal with 'em," Charlie said.

"Well, we ain't!" One of the men lurched forward. He didn't care about the cause of the trouble, he just wanted action.

Charlie swung the pistol hard and the barrel cut through flesh down to the skull as the man collapsed, howling. "Drag him inside," Charlie told McKay.

189

"And lock him up." He turned to the crowd.

Another man, obviously the ring leader, shrugged. "Hell, we though we was doin' you a favor, Marshal. If that's the way you feel, we'll go on back to the saloons."

"You do that," Charlie urged them. He waited until the last of them had drifted back to the bars of the town. He turned to McKay. "How you doin'?"

"Fine, Charlie. Hey, what happened to yore badge?"

"Took a hit there," Charlie said.

"Well, there's a spare in the desk," McKay reminded him.

"I think I'll wear this 'un," Charlie said. "Somehow it appeals to me all bent and twisted like that."

"You reckon we'd both better spend the rest o' the night here?" McKay asked. "That bunch o' drunks might be back."

"No they won't," Charlie said. "I seen this kind o' situation before. A few more drinks and most of 'em will be too far gone to even remember tonight's happenin's. But it wouldn't hurt if you slept in the empty cell jest in case."

"Sure thing," McKay said. "You headin' home now?"

"I reckon," Charlie said wearily. "See you in the mornin'."

Instead of going directly back to the boarding house, however, he made a precautionary stop by the saloons, but this satisfied him that the crowd of drinkers had either thinned out or passed out. Feeling better, he went home.

Matty was alone in the kitchen when he got there. She kissed him. "Coffee?"

"Sure."

190

She poured them each a cup and sat down. "That puts the wraps on the Nolan Edgewater affair, don't it?" she asked.

"Yeah," Charlie answered. "And it turned out to be a hell of a thing, didn't it?" He remembered that only a short time before he had been a hopeless, suicidal drunk and was now a respected lawman again. All this brought on by the death of Nolan Edgewater that ended five years of wasted life for Charles Houston Martell.

"I was thinkin'," Matty said. "Yo're jest like that star on yore vest. Bent some, but still standin' fer what you think is right. The law you believe in was never more firmly established than right here in Caldwell, Charlie."

"Exactly the way Harry Green would have wanted it," Charlie said.

"Who would've thought he'd've died yore friend."

"Me least of all," Charlie said.

"You comin' to bed?" she asked.

"After awhile maybe," Charlie replied.

She got up and kissed him. "G'night, darlin'."

He returned her kiss and sat there in deep thought for a long time. Finally he pushed himself from the table and stood up. A look out the window showed the dawn beginning to break red and glorious. There was no sense in sleeping now. He picked up his hat and left the boarding house.

The town he limped through was his now by virtue of the responsibility he had assumed as well as the standards he had set to guide his life by. Everything was back in control now—even drinking had returned to a pleasant pastime he could take or leave—and to top it off, he had a good woman to share the good and bad of a life that brought back his self-respect.

When Charlie arrived at the office McKay was dozing in a chair. The younger lawman grinned sheepishly at his own sleepiness. "Is the sun comin' up?"

"Jest peekin' over the eastern prairie," Charlie said. He sat at the desk and pulled his record book from the drawer. "I think I'll git started on the report on last night's shootin' and arrests. Gonna be some charges laid down before the judge, too."

"Our work don't never end," McKay said, yawning.

"Don't seem to," Charlie said as the scratching of his pen blended in with the ticking of the wall clock.